Advance Praise
Pilgrim Girl
Diary and Recipes
of her First Year in the New World
by Jule Selbo and Laura Peters

"*Pilgrim Girl* has great writing in the diaries. And the cooking part makes you want to eat and eat…you can really feel like a Pilgrim might."
Students at Westridge School
Pasadena California

"As a young girl, I remember drawing pictures of Pilgrims at Thanksgiving and wondering how they lived. Where did they sleep? How did they speak? And, for goodness sake, what did they EAT? I loved this book and want to make some of the recipes right now! *Pilgrim Girl* is a tasty read indeed."
Emily Squires, Emmy Award winning director of Sesame Street,
Co-Author of Spiritual Places in and around New York City

"*Pilgrim Girl* provides a comprehensive overview of what life was like for the Pilgrims in this fascinating drama. What a unique approach."
Dolores Johnson, writer and illustrator
Children's Book of Kwanzaa, Seminole Diary and Now Let Me Fly

"Like the pilgrims themselves, this book dares to discover new worlds of experience, enlivening history with the flavor of real life. Warm-hearted, witty and wise, *Pilgrim Girl* will enchant readers of all ages."
Jodi Ann Johnson, English Department
Pierce College, California
Nicholl Fellowship in screenwriting winner

"Constance Godwin's diary entries chronicle the hardships and sorrows, as well as the unexpected pleasures and surprises of establishing a home in a new land and trying to meet the basic daily need for healthy and flavorful food. The authentic recipes entice us to experiment and share in Constance's world."
Mary Ann Schroeter, Fifth Grade Reading Teacher
Westridge School, Pasadena California

"Engaging line to social history through cooking. Monthly journal entries of a Pilgrim girl's first year in the New World are brought to life in recreated 17th century recipes, including several for Thanksgiving."
Bruce Rubin, Liberal Studies Department
California State University at Fullerton

Pilgrim Girl

Diary and Recipes
of her First Year in the New World

Pilgrim Girl

Diary and Recipes
of her First Year in the New World

by

Jule Selbo

and

Laura Peters

Pilgrim Girl
Diary and Recipes of her First Year in the New World
©Jule Selbo and Laura Peters 2005

Pilgrim Girl: Diary and Recipes of her First Year in the New World
is a work of fiction. All incidents and dialogue, and
all names and characters, with some exceptions, are products
of the authors' imaginations and are not to be construed as real.
Where historical events or the real-life figures appear, the
situations, incidents and dialogues are entirely imaginary.

ISBN: 1-932993-05-3 (Print Book)
ISBN: 1-932993-06-1 (E-Book)

Library of Congress Number
LCCN: 2005922172

Edited by Star Publish
Cover Design and Illustrations by Mark Winkworth
Interior Design by Mystique Design and Editorial

Published in 2005 by Star Publish

Printed in the United States of America

A Star Publish Book
http://starpublish.com
Nevada, U.S.A. and St. Croix, U.S.V.I.

ACKNOWLEDGEMENTS

We thank the following friends, teachers and colleagues for their support on this project. Nothing is accomplished without a "village" of inspiration. In no particular order they are: Jodi Ann Johnson, Lyn Stimer, Bonna Newman, Robert and Wilkie Stevens, Kristie Leigh Maguire, Lea Schizas, Margaret Danielak, Elaine Post, Jerrilynn Jacobs, Nevena Orbach, Jan Bina, Laurel Thurston, Los Angeles Writers Bloc, Langley Public Library on Whidbey Island, Friends of First Sunday Cooking Group, Captain Jack Winkworth, Susan Merson, Westridge School in Pasadena, Carolyn Howard-Johnson, Ted Larson and Tony and Ronald at Doglight Studios in Los Angeles.

And especially our families

John, Hana, Claire and Rebecca Peters
and
Mark and Lilliana Winkworth

dedicated to our daughters

TABLE OF CONTENTS

INTRODUCTION

Each November when our daughters were in elementary school, the teachers planned a Thanksgiving feast in their classrooms. Every year we, as parents who volunteered to contribute, wished there was a reference we could go to and learn about the Pilgrims' preparation of that feast. What food had they brought with them? What did they grow in their gardens that first year? What fish and game were available and how did they cook it? What hardships, challenges and successes did they experience when trying to feed their bodies and souls that first year?

Finally, we decided to research and write a book ourselves; one that would explore and hopefully answer our questions.

After reviewing numerous primary resources such as ship's logs, diaries from the era and other historical records, we felt that we had a feel for the language and culture of the time. We created the fictional characters of 12-year-old Constance Godwin and her family, with the idea of giving the reader a glimpse into the daily life of New Plymouth. We entwined our fictional family with the survival of the actual passengers on the Mayflower such as the obnoxious boy named Francis Billington and the colony's first Governor, Master Bradford.

We spent a lot of time researching what was eaten on board the Mayflower, what was available to the Pilgrims when they arrived in Massachusetts, and how different seasons introduced new natural foods. When the Native American Squanto entered the Pilgrims' lives, a whole new area of food possibilities was discovered. We found a few recipes and references to food preparation in books on the Mayflower experience and adapted and changed them to suit Constance's mother's creative approach to food. Jule's experience in culinary school allowed her to fashion recipes using, at first, the meager rations available on the Mayflower and then adding the American bounty that became available to the colony. Some recipes are authentic and found in our research. All are dishes that certainly the Pilgrims could have made in their "kitchens" of the time.

Our goal was to create a piece of historically-based fiction that would allow parents and their children a glimpse of what it was like to be a child coming of age in 1620 as well as offer recipes they could use to create meals together throughout the holidays.

Some of the recipes are a bit complex for a child under the age of twelve to attempt alone. We hope parents and grandparents, teachers and friends will enjoy sharing the experience of cooking these recipes with children.

Obviously, young Constance and her family could not avail themselves of such modern conveniences as a refrigerator or an oven with adjustable temperature. But our modern kitchens are well-equipped and so these recipes take advantage of our progress.

Welcome to Constance Godwin's first year in the New World. Enjoy!

Jule Selbo and Laura Peters

FOREWORD

ON SEPTEMBER 6th, in the year 1620, when King James the First ruled Britain, a sailing ship called the Mayflower, carrying 102 passengers and approximately 30 crew members left Plymouth, England. The passengers had plans to begin a new colony in an area called "Virginia" on the continent of North America. Their plans were to change.

All of the passengers were called Pilgrims. Some traveled to find religious freedom; all were looking for a better life.

People who study historical records believe these 50 men, 20 women, and 32 children traveled with the ship's cat and 3 pet dogs. Each man was required to bring enough "victuall" (food) to provide for himself and his family for one year.

Here is a list of what they brought, written as it would have been in 1620, for these be "the usuall proportion the Virginia Company doe bestow upon their Tenents they send."

     8 bushels of meale [wheat]
     2 bushels of pease

2 bushels of Ote-meale
1 gallon of Aqua-vitae [brandy or whisky]
1 gallon of oyle
2 gallons of vineger
Spices and herbes such as Rosemary and Thyme
Dried Fruit
Sugar
Cheese
Bacon
Turnips, Parsnips
Pickled Eggs
Pigs Foote
Smoked ham
Dried Mutton
Dried Sausage
Apples
Nuts
Pickled Cabbage
Lemons
Salted beefe
Salted codfish
Hardtack
Onions
Beer (ale)
Seeds: Meale, Pease, Barley
Goates
Pigs
Chickens
Household implements for a family and six persons
1 Iron pot
1 Kettell
3 Skellets
1 Gridiron
1 Spit
Platters, dishes, spoones of wood

PROLOGUE

Constance Godwin sailed to America on the British ship, the Mayflower, in 1620. She was twelve years old and had much to learn. Her mother set out to teach Constance what she knew and loved to do best – feed and take care of others.

This is the diary of Constance's first year...Of traveling on a ship with nearly nothing to eat...Of landing in the cold winter when food was scarce...Of foraging for food with her Mother...Of cooking over fires and in a homemade rock oven...Of nearly running out of provisions...

And of meeting the Indian Squanto in her first spring in the New World. Squanto became Constance's second teacher in the art of cooking. Squanto taught her how to sow and reap, fish and hunt, and cook the bounty of the New World...

Together with her family, and her old and new friends, Constance joined in the celebration of the very first Thanksgiving.

ARRIVAL

November 1620...Our New Home in Sight

Hail to thee! My name be Constance. God be praised, after 65 days of bobbing about at sea in the Mayflower, blown thither and yon, our ship's mate finally spotted our destination. 'Tis land! And a more beautiful sight than ever I dreamed. I knew there would be no shops, houses, or roads, but the rawness of the wild does amaze me. I scan the woods for signs of the feathered men we have heard tell. I confess I be more relieved than disappointed at not seeing any.

The Elders realized we were blown off course. The Virginia colony we sought is somewhere else indeed. The Elders must take time to get their bearings. So, alas, here we be, but they feel it safest for only small parties of men to go ashore.

I look to the heavens for patience but I am fair jumping in my petticoats to get off this leaky, smelly cork of a boat, especially when time comes each day to fix the daily supper.

As my mother and I stood at the rail, looking at that lovely land, I could see that she was as anxious to disembark as I. She yearned to forage for food that might grow wild, even in the winter. I admit to hubris where my mother's victuals were concerned. She could make the simplest pudding taste extraordinary. While we lived in Holland, she bought foreign spices from the traders and learned to use them with good effect. God forgive me, but I did enjoy the envy of my peers when they ate at my family table!

Those treasured spices are among the things we have packed for this long journey: pepper and ginger from India, cinnamon and cloves from the Indies, a small amount of saffron from Spain, and nutmeg from the Americas.

But even Mother could do little these last two months with our rations of salt beef, salt pork, mutton, dried cod, smoked herring, dried tongue, cheese, oatmeal, stale water and beer. These items keep well on a long voyage, but leave the mind and body craving a fresh peach or a grape. The occasional lemon to prevent the scurvy fares not as well as the tasty puddings of Holland and England I've gone so long without. Dear friend, you can but imagine how I longed to search for food in this new, cold, desolate place.

Mother will cook aboard tonight using our small charcoal brazier, but alas, what be left of any appeal? The men be too occupied with exploring and not enough with bringing us food. So hardtack and oatmeal it be. Hardtack is a sturdy enough bread that can be stored for a long time without spoiling. 'Tis better if you soak it in water or beer to lessen its rock like nature. I include the recipe.

*****

HARDTACK

2 cups of flour
3/4 to 1 cup water
1 tablespoon of lard
6 pinches of salt

Mix ingredients together into a stiff batter, knead several times, and spread the dough on a baking sheet at a thickness of 1/2 inch. Bake for one-half hour at 400°F. Remove from oven, cut dough into 3-inch squares, and punch four holes per row into the dough. Turn dough over, return to the oven and bake another 30 minutes. Turn oven off, leaving door closed. Leave hardtack in the oven until cool.

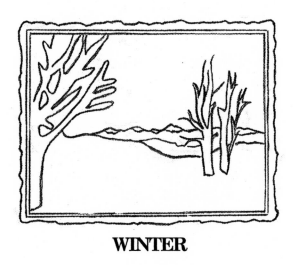

WINTER

December 1620...Anchoring at New Plymouth

God be praised, the men arrived back in the shallop to tell us they have found a safe harbor for which we quickly set sail. We soon set anchor near lands we have named New Plymouth. I heard the Elders say we be far from Virginia and our promised lands, but winter is on us and we have little food stores left so it is decided we settle here. I, for one, yearn to run in an open meadow! But my patience shall have to sustain me a bit longer. We are to stay on ship until our homes be built. The men set out for lumber to build the Common House this very day! There are trees aplenty for chopping. Ready they are, as we all be, to have a shelter on solid land.

This place we shall call home lies on the slope of a hill stretching east towards the coast. A sand bank, 20 paces broad, protects it from the sea. The Elders say there is, to the south but a short distance, a river of fresh water coming from the hills and leading to the sea with fish plentiful enough. The men say that the large size of the trees proves there is good, rich soil for the planting. The planting must wait for this rich soil to thaw, for it is hard with cold now.

Mother, I thank the heavens, saw an opportunity. She gently suggested to Master Bradford that providing good nourishment for the men would aid the building of our Common House. "Feed the body and the spirit quickly follows," she said. She gave me a wink when he did allow that he and the other men were weary of oatmeal and dried beef, and, cook that she is, she may join the men on the shallop boat to land. There she will prepare food for the builders. Blessedly, and most wonderful, she brought me with her! I carried the rations and makings for her Pease Soup. Together we joined the men in the shallop. I waved to my closest friends, Mary and Patience, as the men began rowing. Francis Billington, a boy filled with too much mischief for my liking, glared with envy at me. He wished to be in my place. God forgive me, for I did have smug feelings for my good fortune.

How solid land is! I had almost forgotten the feeling of it. As we set about finding dry enough oak leaves and wood to start the fire, Mother confided that she wanted to see what foods and condiments she might find in this new land. But first to the feeding of the men!

We set a large blaze to cook the food. The heat from it warmed my frozen bones.

Mother sent me to the river with a bucket. Parts of the river were covered with thin ice, but I was able to fill the bucket with cold, fresh water. Though warned against the drinking of it for fear it be contaminated like some of the waters from our old world, after two months of only beer on the Mayflower, I couldn't help but try some. It tasted better than any water I ever had; clean and crisp it was. When I opened my eyes, I was startled to see a face peeping at me from behind a large boulder. When our eyes met, she, for indeed I believe the face belonged to a girl, ducked behind her rock. My voice surprised me with its loudness, for I was startled. "Greetings!" I offered. And waited. Nothing. As I hoisted my bucket of water, she rose again. Her age be hard to tell, but her eyes be brown and curious. Her long dark hair fell to her waist and she was clad in skins. She darted away quickly. My heart was pounding, but for some reason, I did not feel fear.

As I brought the bucket of water back to my mother, I decided to keep this sighting private lest my elders begin to suspect danger and not allow me to be alone. Mother was ready to make the soup upon my return. We also made the fried bread Mother learned to make in Holland to go along with it. I wondered what the Indian girl was to eat that day.

*****

PEASE SOUP

2 cups of split peas
1 ham bone
1 cup chopped sausage
1/2 cup chopped onions
2 cloves chopped garlic
1 large bay leaf
1 teaspoon dried rosemary
1 teaspoon cayenne pepper
2 tablespoons molasses
5 cups vegetable broth
Boiling water

Rinse 2 cups of split peas and pick out any that look shriveled and black-ish. Put the peas in a heavy pot, pour boiling water over them till they are all covered and let them soak for one hour.

Add broth and 5 cups water along with ham bone and bay leaf. Simmer, covered, for two and a half to three hours. Lift out the ham bone. Brown sausage in a separate pan. When the sausage is lightly browned, remove the sausage and pour the fat into a heat-proof bowl, leaving 1 tablespoon left in pan. Brown the chopped onions in the sausage fat.

When the onions are browned, add the chopped garlic for just a minute, do not over-brown garlic, it will taste bitter.

Add the cayenne, rosemary, sausage, onions and garlic to the pot with the peas. Check liquid level, add water if necessary. Simmer, covered, for 1/2 hour. Use a large spoon to take out a few split peas and taste to assure they are tender. (Serves 6-8)

* * * * *

OLY KOEKS

1 cup whole wheat flour
1 cup all purpose flour
1/3 cup raisins or dried cranberries (optional)
1/2 teaspoon salt
2 tablespoons vegetable oil
1/2 cup water
Vegetable oil for frying

Mix flour and salt in a bowl. Add vegetable oil and mix with your fingertips. Add the water and use your hands to mix and gather it into a ball of dough.

Knead the dough, pushing it down and folding it over, adding raisins into each fold. Knead at least 10 minutes until it is very smooth. Cover with a towel or cloth and let it set 30 minutes.

Divide the dough into 12 pieces and roll into balls. Cover again and let them rest 15 minutes.

Heat a cast-iron pan filled one inch deep with vegetable oil until the oil is very hot (375°F). Roll out the balls of dough into circles 5 inches across. They will be very thin. Fry one at a time. They will puff up quickly in the hot oil, turn them over and cook on the other side. Lift out of oil with a strainer, drain on paper towels. Eat while warm.

* * * * *

Mother served the soup and bread and I quickly set about cutting wedges of cheese for the men. They were most grateful and their work seemed to move apace.

Having finished the cooking, Mother tied her foraging bag to her waist and we set out with a knife to search for edibles. Mother pointed out the various bushes and trees as we walked briskly about. She told me they would provide berries in the springtime. How I wish that spring would come.

Soon she stopped before a large tree with scaly and furrowed bark. The tree was leafless but Mother said that joyous she was that this be a black walnut tree. She knelt on the ground and dug into the cold snow at the base of the tree. Shortly her digging afforded a reward. Dark brown-black walnuts that she hoped were not wormed or rotted. We dug all around the tree and found a good many nuts to put in our bag. Mother assured me that with the help of a hammer, we would crack the hard shells and pick out the tender nut meat.

As we boarded the shallop to return to our Mayflower home, Master Brewster came running towards us. He had found vines of grapes and, though the small fruits were frozen and somewhat shriveled, they were a sight that brought me joy. Happily we took all our finds back to the ship.

Those who waited on our ship for our return were glad indeed. As it happened, this was on the eve of the day we celebrate the birth of Our Lord. So it was with added gratitude that we took hammer to the strong walnut shells. We lit a brazier to toast the walnut meat. Mother knew just how much spices and salt to add to make them a treat indeed! Though somewhat gone to vinegar, the grapes were fresh food, which we all ate.

Francis Billington wanted to know all the details of our new home. Because it was a special night and thanks to God we were giving, I put aside my opinion of him and relayed every step I took on the soil of our New World. All but one detail; I did not tell him, or anyone, of my silent meeting of the Indian girl.

January 1621...A New Year Begins in a New Land

The weather has been too cold and windy to forage and cook outdoors and Mother and I must stay aboard the ship. The Common House is near done and I tell Mary and Patience that I dearly long to be within it, for we do share all our secrets. They are near sick with worry for their parents who have not remained strong on the voyage. I try to engage them in other thoughts, especially since I am now to stay aboard the ship with them and tend to the needs of the younger children who have not fallen to the illness. The long days at sea have made the children restless for adventure. To keep their minds from running about when their bodies are still aboard this vessel, we give them chores and try to give rise to their natural competitiveness. One group of boys tries to card more wool than another group of boys. One group of girls shines the cookware brighter than the other. They get much labor done without awareness of tedium! Mother suggests a game of bobbing for pickled eggs. These be the very eggs she pickled before the start of our crossing.

＊＊＊＊＊

PICKLED EGGS

6 hard-boiled eggs
24 whole cloves
2 cups vinegar plus 2 tablespoons
1/2 teaspoon ground mustard
1/2 teaspoon salt
1/2 teaspoon pepper

Shell the hard-boiled eggs and stick 4 cloves into each egg. Boil 2 cups of vinegar. While the vinegar boils, mix the 2 tablespoons cold vinegar with mustard, salt and pepper and add to the boiling vinegar. Put the eggs in a crock or jar and pour boiling vinegar mixture over them. Cover and refrigerate for 2 weeks. Remove the whole cloves before eating.

*****

The weather has abated a bit and the men folk will leave the ship to continue work on land. But still, they believe it is too cold for Mother and me to join them. But I am amazed that trouble-making younker, Francis Billington, has persuaded the men folk that he could be of help to them in their toils. Disappointed for my own fate, I still say to Mary and Patience, good riddance! I will not miss Francis Billington's complaints and teasing. But still, I worry that, with him on land, our homes will never be finished.

There be reasons for my fears, though they were none of Francis Billington's doings. As it happened, the thatch of the Common House caught fire and we all feared its loss. God smiled on us however and the structure remained intact.

Still, aboard our Mayflower ship, troubles did not cease. The weather is forbidding, with much wind and snow. There is much sickness. There be no warm place and we must huddle together. The chickens that have made this journey have ceased laying. Mary, Patience and I warrant their eggs are frozen inside. We have decided to sleep with our hens tonight and hope to warm them enough for some offering, however small. Food remains a constant worry. Our rations continue to deplete. I dream of warm custard, but fear that we must be sustained with what is yet left in our stores. When the weather clears, the men have promised to set about catching fish but for now we must be sustained with the salted cod Mother prepared before we sailed.

I see all shiver and we try to rub our raw hands together for heat, but alas, the chill is great.

Good tidings. Finally today the sun shone and once again I set foot on land. Mary and Patience ventured on the shallop as well. They were amazed that their legs felt odd on solid ground, so used they were to the rocking of the sea.

Mother told us we would make a rock oven in which to cook the fish when God provided it. We dug a round hole in the ground about three feet across and a foot and a half deep. The ground was indeed hard but we did persevere. With some effort, we lined it with fist-sized rocks, keeping the dirt close at hand. We built a fire in the rock saucer and let it burn until the rocks were hot and sizzled when water was dropped on them. Fortunate it was Master Howland approached with a dozen large fish the men had caught. Mother taught me to cut off the fins first so as not to nick myself on their sharpness. We scaled the fish and cleaned them of their entrails and bones and left the rest intact. Mother prepared a fish stifle. She says it is so called because the fish is smothered with vegetables and herbs as it is cooked.

We removed the logs and embers from the rock oven with a shovel, and doused them. After lining the pit of hot rocks with a bed of moistened leaves, Mother placed the fish in a large skillet and put the covered skillet on the stones and smothered it with a damp cover of leaves. Lastly we shoveled the dirt atop and waited with great anticipation for our first fresh catch in the New World.

* * * * *

HADDOCK STIFLE

1 1/2 pounds haddock, cut into bite-
size pieces
4 slices of bacon
1 bay leaf
1 medium onion
1 cup diced parsnips
1/2 cup walnuts
2 cups fish stock or vegetable broth
1 teaspoon dried thyme
1 teaspoon dried rosemary
1/4 teaspoon cayenne pepper
1/2 teaspoon salt
1/2 teaspoon black pepper

Preheat oven to 350°F.

Salt and pepper the fish. Sauté bacon in a pan until barely crisp. Remove bacon. Sauté the vegetables in bacon fat. Take out half the vegetables and place in an oven-proof casserole dish. Arrange the fish atop the vegetables, crumble bacon and herbs on top of the fish. Cover with the remaining vegetables. Pour in enough stock to barely cover the layers. Cover the casserole and bake for 30 minutes.

* * * * *

Mother also planned to cook fish on the open fire and for that we set up a spit from which to hang a pot. Oh, to stand next to that fire and imagine the bounty of the New World that was soon to fill our shrunken stomachs. If only this nourishment could bring health to those who suffered on our long journey. I prayed with Mary and Patience for their parents' good fortune. They be weak, but surely good weather and food will bring new color to their cheeks.

* * * * *

CARP BOILED IN A POT

One whole gutted carp, skinned
1/4 pound salt pork, cubed
3 cups water
1/2 teaspoon salt
Dash of pepper

Salt and pepper the fish. Sauté the salt pork until browned. Lay the fish atop the salt pork, pour water (enough to cover the fish) and salt over the fish. Bring the water to a boil and boil until cooked through, around 20 minutes.

* * * * *

Mother instructed me to save every scrap of fish for she wanted to make fish cakes. They could be cooked and kept for a few days in case the weather again forced us to take cover.

* * * * *

FISH CAKES

3 cups cooked, flaked fish
3 cups diced bread
1/2 cup diced onion
2-3 eggs, beaten
1 tablespoon dried thyme or dill
1 teaspoon pepper
1/2 cup vegetable oil
1/2 cup flour

Brown onions in a tablespoon of oil. Add them to fish, bread, eggs, herbs and pepper. Mold the mixture into patties. Heat the oil in a skillet until it is hot, dust the patties lightly with flour and fry in the oil, 5 minutes on each side or until cooked through.

*****

January 31, 1621

A very special day indeed, my mother teased me. Surprised I was, when on this, my thirteenth birthday, Master Brown tuned up his fiddle in the Common House and those of us feeling well enough danced a jig. Mother prepared her delicious Sausage Pie for our supper and crowned the day of merriment with not one, but two sweet puddings.

*****

SAUSAGE PYE

CRUST:
3 cups flour
1 cup vegetable shortening or lard
1 egg
1 teaspoon white vinegar
1/4 teaspoon salt
3-4 tablespoons cold water
1 egg white for brushing crust

FILLING:
2 pounds sausage meat
1 medium onion, diced
2 turnips or potatoes, diced
1 teaspoon dried thyme
1 teaspoon dried rosemary
1/2 teaspoon salt
1/4 teaspoon pepper
2 tablespoons whiskey
1 large bay leaf
1 1/2 cup broth made from ham bone
3 tablespoons flour

TO MAKE THE CRUST: In a medium size bowl, sift the flour and salt together. Add the shortening and with your fingers, mix with the flour until the mixture feels grainy, like a coarse cornmeal. Mix the egg and vinegar together and blend into the flour mixture. Add just enough water so that the dough barely holds together, not sticky. Press the dough together into a ball and cover completely with a barely damp towel. Let it set in the refrigerator for an hour. After the dough has rested, roll it out with a rolling pin until it is about a quarter of an inch thick and line the bottom of a pie shell with half the crust.

Preheat oven to 375°F.

Pre-bake the bottom crust for fifteen minutes or until it is golden brown. Remove from the oven.

TO MAKE THE FILLING: Put the broth in a saucepan. Add the bay leaf. Bring to a simmer.

While that is simmering, chop the sausage and brown it in a frying pan. Remove the sausage to a plate to drain. Brown onions in the sausage drippings, add the diced turnip or potato and the herbs, salt and pepper and whiskey. Continue cooking for a few more minutes till the alcohol burns off. Add the cooked sausage.

Put the flour into a separate bowl and slowly add 1/3 cup warm broth, stirring continually until the mixture is smooth and contains no lumps. Add 1/3 cup more warm broth to thin the mixture, then add into sauce pan with the rest of the broth. Remove the bay leaf. Pour the broth over the sausage mixture and stir together. Fill the pre-baked bottom crust.

Cover with the top crust. Brush the top crust with egg white and make three cuts into it so that the pie can vent while baking.

Bake for 45 minutes or until the top crust is golden brown.

★ ★ ★ ★ ★

STEAMED PUDDING

1 cup flour
2 cups chopped suet
2 cups raisins
2 cups dates or currants
1 grated nutmeg
1 teaspoon ground cinnamon
1/2 teaspoon ground cloves
1 teaspoon ground ginger
1 teaspoon salt
6 tablespoons molasses or sugar
7 egg yolks
7 egg whites, whipped to soft peaks
1/2 cup whiskey
1/4 cup water or cream
3 cups bread crumbs

Combine the oil, dried fruit and spices. Sprinkle with part of the flour and salt and stir. Add the remaining flour, mix well. Add the molasses, egg yolks, whiskey, water and bread crumbs. Whip the egg whites until they reach the soft peak stage and fold them lightly into mixture. Pour into an oiled gallon mold and steam for 6 hours. The pudding must be cooked slowly so that the suet has time to melt and incorporate its flavor.

* * * * *

CHEWET PYE

CRUST:
1 1/2 cups flour
1/2 cup vegetable shortening or lard
1 egg
1 teaspoon white vinegar
1/4 teaspoon salt
1-2 tablespoons cold water

FILLING:
1 cup raisins
1 cup pitted dates
2 cups water or apple juice
1/2 cup molasses or sugar
2 tablespoons vegetable oil or butter
2 tablespoons flour
2 egg yolks
1 tablespoon whiskey
1/2 cup walnuts

TO MAKE THE CRUST: In a medium size bowl, sift the flour and salt together. Add the shortening and with your fingers, mix with the flour until the mixture feels grainy, like a coarse cornmeal. Mix the egg and vinegar together and blend into the flour mixture. Add just enough water so that the dough barely holds together, you don't want to make it sticky. Press the dough together into a ball and cover completely with a barely damp towel. Let it set in the refrigerator for an hour. After the dough has rested, roll it out with a rolling pin until it is about a quarter of an inch thick. Line the bottom of a pie shell with the crust.

This pie only uses a bottom crust. Pre-bake it for 15 minutes at 375°F or until lightly browned.

Put the raisins, dates and water into a saucepan and bring to a boil over medium heat. Add the molasses. Cool slightly. Stir in oil and flour gently, make sure it is well combined. Cook over low heat until the flour is combined. Remove from the heat. Beat egg yolks and whiskey together, add to mixture along with the walnuts, stir until well combined. Cool the filling, then put into the baked pie shell and bake for 20 minutes at 350°F.

February 1621...A Home of Our Own

God be praised. Father has completed our house and we no longer call the Mayflower home. Now Father has set himself to work at night to fashion a table, a stool and new trenchers. This is the dream we dreamed for near six months. Due to God's blessings, Mother, Father and I have remained of good health though our brethren perish daily. We have taken in Mary and Patience, whose parents were not so fortunate. I easily call them sisters now. In their prayers every night, Mary and Patience ask God to assure their parents, who He holds now in his hands, that they be safe in the New World.

My new sisters and I helped Mother prepare what food we have at our own hearth. Mother teaches us her secrets for tasty breads that we will be able to eat and soak in our soups. We passed much of the day baking, which gave the benefit of a warm house! We could hardly wait for supper that eve.

✶ ✶ ✶ ✶ ✶

BEATEN BISCUITS

4 cups unbleached flour
1/2 cup shortening or lard
1/2 cup cold water
Pinch of salt
1/4 teaspoon sugar

Preheat oven to 400°F.

Put flour in a bowl with shortening, salt and sugar. Mix with your hands until well-blended. Pour in water and mix well with fork until the flour sticks together. Place dough on a flat board on a strong table. Put a damp towel under the board so it won't slip. Pound dough with a kitchen weight for about 20 minutes or until dough looks smooth and glossy.

Pinch off a piece of dough and form each piece into a ball about 2 inches in diameter. Place balls on cookie sheets and prick tops with the tines of a fork.

Bake biscuits for 20 minutes or until golden brown. Serve with jam, syrup or butter. Makes about 2 dozen biscuits.

How easily we stood to eat our supper, napkins draped across our shoulders, as is our custom. Father sat on his newly carved stool to give the blessing and we admired his handiwork. We long to appease our hunger. And finally our first feast in our home was tasted. Our hands brought food to our mouths, a bit too greedily for God's eyes I fear.

After supper and the cleaning, Father read the Bible to us and listened to our psalms. Mary and Patience have prodigious memories for they know their verses word for word and my father advises me to learn from their example. And so I recited psalms even as I worked and hoped they would be heard as prayers for continued good fortune.

God heard my prayers. The next day Master Howland, who be a bachelor, brought to Mother five rabbits he found in the traps he set but one day before. As my mother was admired for her skills in cooking, Master Howland was wise to share with us his rabbits. Mother examined the catch and exclaimed with pleasure at the narrow clefts in the lips and sharp smooth claws. When I bid her tell me why, she explained that this showed a young and therefore tasty rabbit. How my mouth did water. And even when Master Howland suggested his nephew, Francis Billington, join us, my anticipation was no less. The truth was, Francis was so enamored of the sweet taste of the rabbit he did not have one annoying word to say all evening. Mary, Patience and I were relieved.

✦ ✦ ✦ ✦ ✦

ROASTED RABBIT

MARINADE:
1 cup onion
8 cups red wine vinegar
4 cups water
1/2 pound bacon
1/2 cup parsley
3 bay leaves
1 teaspoon dried thyme
1 teaspoon dried basil
1/4 cup whole cloves
1/8 cup allspice berries
1/4 teaspoon mace
6 cloves crushed garlic
1 tablespoon peppercorns
1 cleaned rabbit, cut into pieces

Sauté bacon, put aside. Drain and reserve all but 2 tablespoons bacon fat. Sauté the onions in the bacon fat till they are browned. Add the vinegar and water and simmer for one hour. Strain and cool. Pour over rabbit.

Marinate for 24 to 48 hours.

Preheat oven to 350°F. Take the rabbit pieces out of the marinade and dry them with a towel. Dip them in flour. Brown until golden in bacon fat. Put rabbit pieces in an oven-proof dish.

Sauté remaining cup of onions in 1 tablespoon bacon fat.

Cover the rabbit with onions, add marinade and bring to a boil on top of the stove. Cover and put in oven for one and a half hours or until tender. Season with salt and pepper.

*****

This February night was dire cold. Mary, Patience and I slept tight together on our pine needle bedding near the fire. We wondered if spring would ever come to this part of the world. Mother says it will, but it seems as if it will be forever winter. How I long for the thaw.

SPRING

March 1621...Squanto Joins Us

Truth be told, I was fair amazed by the sight of a skin naked savage arriving in our midst. As Goody Brewster whisked me away, lest I see more than I already had, I heard the man utter in the King's tongue, "Hello, Englishmen!"

He stayed the night, speaking at length with the elders. I learned by eavesdropping, God forgive me, that his name was Samoset and he was of the Pemaquid. He had learned to speak our language from trappers and settlers.

The following day Samoset returned with another savage, this one donning overgarments, named Squanto. He, too, speaks English he learned as a slave. He also speaks the language of the Spanish monk who captured him. His hardships as a boy in Spain and England were mighty, but he at last gained his freedom, only to return to this location, which was the site of his Patuxet village. How distraught he must have been to learn that all his people had died from disease the previous year.

God's hand must surely have played a part in sending this man. Squanto seems to pity our ignorance at the simplest tasks. He teaches us with such kindness and patience as I have ever seen. He shows us winter roots to dig and the pots of dried beans and corn he buried for winter storage. There were buried treasures of hickory nuts, onions, and currants, too. He was so generous in sharing, my mother near cried in gratitude.

One morning, Squanto took us to a grove of trees that bore special markings. He cut a "V" shaped slash in the trunk of the first tree. We were surprised to see a watery brown sap begin to flow. Squanto quickly tied a nearly hollowed out log, fashioned as a bucket, to catch the liquid. He followed the same procedure with each tree. In the evening he brought back to camp two full buckets of the liquid. He told Mother how his tribe placed hot stones into the wooden buckets to boil the sap, but he would take advantage of our iron pots over the fire for the boiling of the substance. The sap thickened into syrup over the heat. It was so sweet I closed my eyes to remember its taste always. While the weather is cool, we can keep some of the sap as syrup, but the burden of his collections will be poured into the molds he fashions even now out of wood. The syrup will be preserved as Cake Sugar. If we had lived in this wilderness another hundred years, would we have found this treasure without Squanto? I think not!

Squanto bakes a bread from his stores of dried corn. He calls this corn an Indian name, maize.

Seeing his bread-making skill, Mother determined to follow his instruction. He does look pleased to teach such an interested pupil, his brown skin setting off his white teeth and his smile most warm. I am forever thankful his time enslaved by the Spanish did not create ill will towards us. Truly he knows the meaning of forgiveness better than some Englishmen.

* * * * *

MAPLE CORNBREAD

1 1/3 cups flour
2/3 cup cornmeal
1/2 teaspoon salt
3 teaspoons baking powder
1/3 cup maple syrup
1/2 cup vegetable oil
2 eggs, slightly beaten

Mix the dry ingredients thoroughly. Add the oil and eggs. Stir until well mixed but do not beat. Pour into a greased 9x9 inch baking pan. Bake at 425°F for 25 minutes.

* * * * *

A pudding, made from cornmeal that could be made in short time, was Squanto's next lesson. Mother stood by his side so as not to miss one part of the learning...

* * * * *

HASTY PUDDING

6 cups boiling water
1 teaspoon salt
1 cup yellow cornmeal
1/4 cup maple syrup

Bring the water to a rapid boil in a heavy covered pot. Add the salt, then add the cornmeal slowly, stirring all the time to avoid lumps. Continue stirring until the cornmeal thickens, about 5 minutes. Turn the heat down low and cover the pot. Add the maple syrup. Continue to simmer, stirring several times, for about 30 minutes.

This can be eaten plain or can be covered with milk or cream or even topped with nuts or fruit.

* * * * *

BROWNED HASTY PUDDING

1 portion hasty pudding
4 tablespoons flour
4 tablespoons bacon fat

Make the Hasty Pudding, add 4 tablespoons flour to the hot mixture and stir well. Pour the mush into an oiled loaf pan and chill overnight. Cut the mush into 1/4 inch thick pieces, drenched in flour and brown in bacon fat over a low heat, about 15 minutes a side. This can be served with butter, maple syrup or fruit preserves.

* * * * *

For the first night since we set foot on the land of the New World, I slept with a belly as full as I had once had in Holland.

As the days lengthen, Squanto takes us to find nuts, roots of wild beans, and shows us how to get honey from the bees. Mary, Patience and I beg Mother to use honey in every dish but Mother warns that an ounce of pleasure could provide a pound of bellyache. She set us to the task of making a vegetable compote. Squanto oversaw our efforts, saying it was his favorite meal.

* * * * *

SUCCOTASH

1 cup dried red beans
1 cup corn kernels
1/2 cup diced onion
2 tablespoon bear grease or butter
1/2 teaspoon salt
1/4 teaspoon pepper

Soak the dried beans in water overnight. Put in a saucepan and cover with water. Bring to a boil. Reduce heat, cover the saucepan and simmer until the beans are tender, about 30 minutes. Add the corn kernels and simmer for 5 more minutes. Drain the vegetables. Melt the butter or bear grease in a sauté pan, brown the onion. Add the beans and corn and salt and pepper. Stir together until vegetables are coated and almost brown. Check seasoning and serve.

* * * * *

Squanto quickly showed the men the best places to hunt. He knew where to walk so as to send the largest geese my eyes hath ever beheld into the air over the shores. At least one felt the aim of the musket and will not finish his journey as he is the centerpiece of our dinner this night. This one goose serves many purposes as we saved the fat drippings for stews, pottages and puddings. Mary, Patience and I could not help but giggle with joy as we smelled the roasting bird. God forgive us, we do enjoy flesh eating days. We ponder that it be strange that since God does provide our joy, we still ask his forgiveness for enjoying his gifts. Patience, who likes to make questions of everything, wonders if we are assuming too much that He thinks of us as individual girls and sends blessings that fit our specific needs. But I must admit it gives me fair comfort to think God is knowing each of us so well that his blessings are determined by our needs.

*****

ROASTED GOOSE WITH STUFFING

1 goose (9 to 12 pounds)
Salt

FOR THE STUFFING:
1 cup dried apple, diced
10 dried figs, quartered
2 cups crumbled corn bread
1/2 cup walnuts, chopped
Salt
Pepper
2 teaspoons dried sage
2/3 cup chicken broth

FOR THE GRAVY:
1-2 tablespoons flour
1 1/2 cups reserved goose broth
1 tablespoon bear grease or butter

Remove the neck and gizzards from the goose, put in saucepan with the water and simmer, partially covered for several hours until reduced to 2 cups. This will be your broth. Salt to taste.

Mix all the stuffing ingredients. Salt and pepper to taste. Fill the cavity of the goose and close the cavity with skewers or with twine. Roast at 325°F degrees, breast side down for one and a half hours, drawing off the fat as it accumulates. Turn the goose over, roast for another hour and a half. Check to see if the juices run clear, when they do, the bird is done. Remove from the heat and let it rest on a platter.

TO MAKE A GRAVY: Pour off all but one tablespoon of the fat, sprinkle 1 to 2 tablespoons of flour into the pan. Set the roasting pan over low heat and stir for a minute, scraping up the browned bits. Add the bear grease or butter and the broth (from the goose / neck) and whisk until smooth. Stir over medium heat until gravy reduced to the desired thickness. Season with salt and pepper.

*****

SQUANTO'S QUAIL

8 quail
8 sprigs of rosemary
8 tablespoons vegetable oil or butter
Salt
Pepper
3 medium onions, sliced
1 cup apple juice
8 tablespoons brandy

Clean the birds and put a spring of rosemary and salt inside each of them. Rub one tablespoon of oil or butter over each bird, salt and pepper lightly. Place them in a roasting pan on top of the sliced onions; don't let them touch each other. Add the apple juice to the pan. Roast at 400°F for 45 minutes, basting occasionally. When done, remove the quail to a platter, pour the brandy into the pan and boil about a minute to burn off the alcohol. Pour over the quail and serve immediately.

April 1621...The Mayflower Leaves and Spring Arrives

The last of our homes were but barely built when, on the fifth day of this month, our ship the Mayflower left for the long voyage back to England taking a few of our remaining number with her. God's speed and safe journey to her and all her inhabitants!

As merciless as the winter has been, I could not endure another sojourn aboard that vessel, especially with Spring bringing buds to every tree.

This New World be beautiful. Buds of pink, blue, white and yellow bring color to every meadow and hillside. The sea has calmed and its blue reflects the clearest sky. Each morning the world feels fresh and new; so different from the sooty and most crowded Holland and England. Mary, Patience and I gathered many flowers to adorn our table. Mary told me that she did press many young flowers in the family Bible so we could always remember this first Spring.

As we gathered the flowers, I did spy again the Indian girl I saw the first day at the river's edge. I had wondered if we would meet again. She watched us from high in a blossom filled tree. Silent and motionless she was, though she did smile at me once again. Her face and body were so framed by the flowers that I think I shall call her Blossom. I wonder how she is called in truth, but am well satisfied with the name I have given her for the time being. I kept the secret of my sighting from Mary and Patience, believing they would make a fuss and feeling Blossom did not want to be known. I did manage a wee wave to her as we left the meadow. She stared at me with wide eyes, but I did think she knew I was saying hello.

Not a soul be idle these days as Squanto instructs the men on how to plant the corn. He made them wait until the oak bud had burst and the leaves of oak grew to be the size of a mouse ear. Squanto said this is the signal it is time to plant. He led the men to build mounds with three herring fish per mound to enrich the soil. He promised good yield for following his instructions. The corn is planted. The men also began the family gardens of cabbages, parsnips, radishes, lettuce, melons, carrots, beets and skirrets. Summer may indeed be full of food, but that is still some time away.

Now, the shad be running. 'Tis a blessing my mother has an imagination where the cooking of this bony fish be concerned.

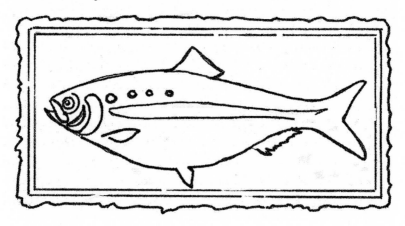

SHAD

Boned shad
Salt
Pepper
Lemon juice
Oil or butter
Cayenne pepper
Walnuts

Grill on one side for 12 minutes. It will be nicely browned. Turn it over and grill for another 10 minutes. Spread oil or butter over the hot fish, sprinkle with cayenne pepper salt and chopped walnuts.

* * * * *

SHAD IN APPLE CIDER

2 pounds shad
Lemon juice
Salt
Pepper
4 tablespoons cider vinegar
1 cup fresh bread crumbs
4 tablespoons oil or butter, melted

Place the sides of shad, skin side down, in one layer, in a buttered dish. Squeeze lemon juice over them and season with salt and pepper. Pour the cider vinegar around the fish. Bring to a simmer on top of the stove, then put under the broiler for 10 minutes, basting a few times with the liquid. Toss the bread crumbs with the oil or melted butter, put under the broiler again for about 2 minutes until lightly browned on top.

61

May 1621...Living Off the Land

As I gathered the ashes of the hearth, I truly counted my blessings. To have solid earth beneath my feet and this house to clean, I am truly fortunate. As my mother sat to spin, Mary, Patience and I set about our chores.

Mary has taken on the teaching of the youngest children their numbers and letters. Patience is dedicated to keeping our house free from dust and spiders, using a turkey wing for her efforts. I prefer varied tasks, such as saving the grease from the morning's fare and collecting the ashes to store in their bin, so that later I can marvel, as I always do, at Mother's skill at making soap. She knows just how to leach the ashes from the fire and add the bear grease for the cleansing soap.

Since the day be warm, I took the bedding out to air. As I hung the quilts on the ropes Father strung from tree to tree, I saw Francis and another smaller boy, Harold, approach Mary's group of students. Francis fair pushed the reluctant Harold towards Mary and exclaimed that his parents want him to be book learned. Mary had other children make a space for Harold and offered to Francis a perch as well. He scuffed his shoe in the dirt, saying he was not interested, but I noticed he neither sat nor left.

I filled my lungs with the fresh air, then re-entered our wee house to set about cleaning the soot from the walls that we may have a home clean for God to dwell. After the walls glowed, I took kettle, pot and skillet outside to put some shine on them. As I worked, I noticed that Francis was now sitting with the group. He had, indeed, alighted right next to Mary who seemed more than a little attentive to him. That she should want to give attention freely to Francis Billington did make me wonder.

I deposited the glimmering pots in the house and went to fetch water for truly I wanted to stretch my legs before helping Mother set about the making of the supper for the men. The men continue to toil in the building of our community and in the field and require nourishing food at the end of their day.

The sea contains many gifts of food. We spend much time catching its fruits. Eel, scallops, oysters, mackerel, cod and clam grace our trenchers daily. Squanto showed us the secrets of the oysters. If the oyster shell is not closed as tight as a newborn's fist, then the oyster may be spoiled and should not be eaten. This vexes Mary, Patience and me as it be extremely difficult to pry open the coarse shell of a healthy, live oyster when it be sealed tightly. Once opened, we rinse the meat in the shell in cold water to make sure shell bits and sand are cleaned off. Squanto says that female oysters should be fried and male oysters should be stewed but I am hard put to tell them apart.

*****

GRILLED OYSTERS IN THE SHELL

Put oysters on a seasoned plank. Place on a low rack over hot coals until the shells pop open.

* * * * *

Squanto explained that unlike oysters, which can be eaten raw, mussels must be cooked. Mother had me scrub the mussel shells with a hard brush and cut the beards off with a knife.

* * * * *

STEAMED MUSSELS

1 onion, chopped
10 large cloves garlic, chopped
1 tablespoon vegetable oil
2 pounds mussels in the shell
4 cups fish or vegetable broth
1/2 cup bread crumbs

In a deep, heavy pot, sauté the onion in the oil, add the garlic, sauté for another minute. Add the broth. When the liquid boils, add the cleaned mussels and cover the pot. When the mussels open (about 5-8 minutes) they are done. Take the mussels out, put in bowls. Add the bread crumbs to the broth to thicken it, pour the broth over the mussels. It's best to eat with your hands, pulling the mussels from their shells.

* * * * *

BAKED MUSSELS

Mussels
Vegetable Oil

Preheat the oven to 450°F. Place well-cleaned mussels in a large oiled pan, drizzle more oil over them. Put into the oven and bake until the shells open.

* * * * *

Indeed, I enjoy the eating of just about everything God provides. But I must consider the amount of work to get one clam ready for the eating before I exclaim to Mother how nice a clam might be for supper. Clams be so sandy. While still in the shell they need such scrubbing as to wear off my palms. Then they must be soaked in fresh water, and the water replaced a few times. Thence they must be moved to a large pot of fresh water with one palm full of salt and soaked for another three hours. Squanto throws in a handful of cornmeal during the last soak to be sure and draw out all the sand. The waiting for them just to be clean is beyond my endurance! If any clams rise to the surface of the water and float, we know they must be bad and chuck them straight away. Indeed, if their shells be opened, they are chucked. Only the tightly closed get another fresh water rinse before cooking.

* * * * *

STEAMED LONG-NECK CLAMS

Place a small amount of salted water in the bottom of a heavy pot. Place a rack on the bottom of the pot. Add the clams. Cover the pot, and steam clams over moderate heat until they open, usually about 5 to 10 minutes.

*****

THE REAL CLAMBAKE

Start preparations about 4 hours before you want to eat. Dig a sandpit about one foot deep and three and a half feet across. Line it with smooth round rocks. Build a fire over the rock surface and feed it for 3 hours while rocks are heating. Gather seaweed, rinse it several times and soak in fresh water for 45 minutes.

3 quarts salted water
10 turnips/parsnips
1 pound chicken
2 large lobsters
4 shucked corn on the cob
1 pound clams in the shell

Line an iron pot with the seaweed and heat on the hot rocks. Add the salted water and the chopped vegetables and let simmer for 15 to 20 minutes. Add the cut-up chicken pieces and simmer for another 15 minutes. Add the quartered lobsters, cook for 10 minutes. Add the shucked corn, cook for 10 more minutes. Add the cleaned and soaked clams in their shells. Cover and steam until the clams are open, about 5 to 10 minutes.

This morning, I watched as the men brought up the dark mottled blue-green lobsters from the sea, laughing as they hoisted each lobster by hand to guess the weight. If a man judged a lobster to be less than two pounds, he tossed it back to grow. Two pounds and over, and he looked on the underside of each creature for the soft, leathery fin-like appendages of the female, found where the body and tail meet. On the male, these appendages are bony. Though the female has the finer flavor, the men threw some back lest we not have any females to make more lobster later.

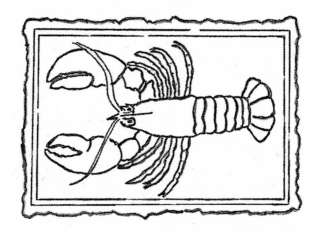

BOILED LOBSTER

Place a thin towel or cloth in the bottom of a heavy pot, put live lobster on top of it. Cover with salted water. Bring the water to a boil and boil for 5 minutes. Reduce the heat and simmer for about15 minutes.

Drain. Serve at once or plunge into cold water to cool quickly to eat the lobster cold.

*****

GRILLED LOBSTER

Marinate lobster in herbs and oil and onion or shallots for 3 hours. Remove with scissors or knife the soft undercover of the lobster tail so that the meat can be seen. Slightly crack the hard upper shell with a cleaver so that the tails will lie flat. Rub the exposed meat with oil. Grill about 4 inches above fire or coals for about 5 minutes a side.

*****

BLUEFISH

1 onion
3 tablespoons vegetable oil
2 tablespoons thyme, basil, cumin
2 teaspoons white vinegar
1 teaspoon sugar
Salt
Pepper
1 cup white wine
2 pounds bluefish fillet

Heat oil in heavy saucepan, add onion and sauté. Add wine and herbs and bring to a boil. Add the water, vinegar, sugar and bring to boil again. Add salt and pepper to taste. Preheat oven to 400°F. Lay the bluefish fillets in one layer in a slightly oiled shallow baking dish. Salt and pepper them lightly, pour hot liquid over them, cover and bake for 15-20 minutes.

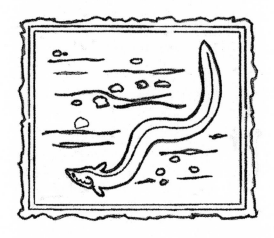

Squanto shows us where the eel can be discovered and assures it is good for eating. Its capture is of great interest. Squanto showed us how to beat the eel from the mud. What a blessing it is that he rests with us! An eel, Squanto showed us, requires a whack on the head for the killing. Then it must be peeled of its skin if one is to enjoy its flesh.

* * * * *

EEL IN A COFFIN

CRUST:
3 cups flour
1 cup vegetable shortening or lard
1 egg
1 teaspoon white vinegar
1/4 teaspoon salt
3-4 tablespoons cold water
1 egg white for brushing crust

FILLING:
1 pound eel cut into three inch pieces
1 pound potatoes, sliced thin
3 medium onions, sliced thin
2 tablespoons flour
Salt
Pepper
1/8 pound salt pork, diced
1 cup milk

TO MAKE THE CRUST: In a medium size bowl, sift the flour and salt together. Add the shortening and with your fingers, mix with the flour until the mixture feels grainy, like a coarse cornmeal. Mix the egg and vinegar together and blend into the flour mixture. Add just enough water so that the dough barely holds together, not sticky. Press the dough together into a ball and cover completely with a barely damp towel. Let it set in the refrigerator for an hour. After the dough has rested, roll it out with a rolling pin until it is about a quarter of an inch thick and line the bottom of a pie shell with half the crust.

Preheat oven to 400°F.

Cool. Toss the filling ingredients together and pile into the pie shell. Cover with the top crust and vent the crust. Bake in the oven for 10 minutes, reduce heat to 350°F and bake for 1 hour.

* * * * *

71

EEL GRILLED WITH HERBS

1 pound eel
4 tablespoons vegetable oil
Pepper
Sage or Rosemary sprigs
Salt

Cut the eels in 3-4 inch pieces, wipe them with a damp cloth. Blend the oil, herbs and a pinch of salt together, dip the eel pieces in the oil mixture, place eel on a grill about 4 inches above very high heat.

Grill about 10 minutes, turn the pieces. Baste with seasoned oil and grill 10 more minutes, until golden brown.

* * * * *

MACKEREL STIFLE

1 large onion
1 tablespoon oil
1 cup parsnips
1 cup green beans
1 cup corn
1 bay leaf
3/4 cup white wine
1 teaspoon thyme
1 teaspoon rosemary
1 teaspoon salt
4 pounds mackerel fillets

Sauté chopped onion in oil. Add the parsnips, beans and corn, and bay leaf. Sauté for one minute. Add the wine and stir in chopped herbs and salt. Simmer over gentle heat for 20 minutes, then remove the bay leaf.

Arrange mackerel in an oiled baking dish in one layer, cover with vegetables and liquid. Bake at 400°F for 25 to 30 minutes.

June 1621...Blossom, Bread and Summer

Food! Mary, Patience and I pray to God that He does not think us gluttons for we do crave every day the savories and welcome the variety of fresh vegetables available to us. Memories of hard times aboard ship and the long winter mean we can never take food again for granted. Perhaps all we have suffered will, in part, atone in His eyes.

At last we have fresh cabbage, beets, turnips, lettuces, radishes and parsnips. The beans, onions and squash begin to ready. We have much eel still, as well as rabbit. A deer approaching our garden is sure to be apprehended and prepared for a venison dinner. What Mother can do with all these ingredients!

We have planted twenty acres of corn, six in wheat, barley, rye and peas. The corn and rye fare particularly well. As do mosquitoes which seem to find my flesh delectable. Sensing my discomfort, Mother had me gather lavender for salves against my tormentors. Mother does remind me that eating brewer's yeast will aggrieve insects thirsty for my blood, more than any salve. I press my lips together thinking of that repugnant taste and pray the lavender will suffice.

As the fruit trees begin to bear, Squanto shows us how to pinch the fruit off heavily laden branches. At first the elders protested that we need all the food God sees fit to bring us, but Mother allowed Squanto's superior knowledge of this new land and they chose to follow his counsel. So we leave fruit aplenty at the tops of the trees as gifts for the birds, then thin the offerings on the lower branches. Instead of six peaches to one branch, there be but three. Squanto says the flesh of the peach will be thicker and sweeter for this care.

Mary, Patience and I started our day by plucking a few of the riper onions from the underground, lettuce from the earth's surface and then climbing the trees to select the ripest cherries. From the highest branches, I teased that we had moved up in the world over the course of our day! Weary from our day's collection, we rested against the trunk of the bountiful tree. How we enjoyed the warmth of the late afternoon sun! I was sucking a tart cherry when I noticed Blossom, the young Indian girl who I, in my mind, called friend. She spied on us from behind a nearby tree.

As fortune would have it, Squanto happened along at that moment. Quietly I told him of Blossom, the news of whom Mary and Patience were anxious to learn. They scolded me for not telling of her existence sooner. Squanto called a name in his own language, which caused the girl to start and nearly run away. But Squanto coaxed her further and she walked in our direction. I was well amazed when Squanto told me her name, in her own tongue, meant Squash Flower or Blossom! She stood close to Squanto and smiled shyly. Mary offered her a cherry, which she did not eat. Mary took a bite of a cherry to show how she hoped Blossom would enjoy hers. Blossom bit into her cherry and Mary smiled, commenting she had made a new friend. I was not to be out done, therefore I took a bite of one of our onions. The fumes did make my eyes water, but I offered it to her in the name of friendship, smiling through my tears. Blossom, too, took a large bite and her eyes pooled with tears. This caused us all to laugh and quickly eat some cherries.

Then, of a sudden, she did dart into the woods. Mary, Patience and I were exchanging puzzled looks when we saw Francis hurrying towards our number, breathlessly asking who had departed.

I teased that it was but a deer, to which Mary and Patience emphatically agreed. Squanto but smiled. I did wonder if he was confused by our fabrication or if he understood our desire to keep Blossom for our special friend alone.

Francis explained that our mother bid us come home for she was to begin the making of the bread.

We all looked at one another and knew the joy the other felt at the certainty that within a week we would be sinking out teeth into Mother's chewy, soft bread.

Mother, apron covering her over garments, was already up to her elbows in flour and dough when we arrived. "'Tis finally warm enough for the rising of the dough!" she joyfully exclaimed. Squanto informed my Mother he was most anxious to learn this ancient art from her.

She brought Squanto up to date with her work so far in preparing to make bread. A full week has gone by since she made a mixture of warm water and flour and set it aside to ferment. We smelled the mixture. It was of sour state and we did wrinkle our noses. Mother was not perturbed, she pointed with pride to the frothy bubbles in the mixture. She stated that this was a mixture called "a starter" and would make it possible for us to make bread that would rise and become soft and airy in middle, unlike the oly keoks and hardtack breads and cornbreads. The wild yeast in the air had helped form this frothy sour mixture. She had added the starter to a dough mixture and now we were to work the combination on a board as she spoke. She reminded us all to cover our hands with flour to keep the dough from sticking to them.

Mother said this was the wonderful and mysterious part of bread! The very air God gives us helps to make the staff of life.

Mother proudly put the bowl with the remaining starter to the side. She said it would last all year long if properly stored. She moved our kneaded dough to bowls, covered them with linen clothes and set them by the hearth. Mother told us it would take time for the dough to rise and then it would be baked in the brick oven Father built in our own garden. Mother told how bread has been made this way for centuries, even as far back as Egypt 4000 BC.

Mother also said when beer-making commences, she will be able to get yeast by using the froth that forms at the top of fermenting ale or beer. This yeast is called barm. Barm can be mixed in a large bowl with flour, then covered with a linen cloth and blanket to keep warm overnight. One can add barm to the other bread ingredients on baking day to create a loaf of God's blessed mystery.

* * * * *

SIMPLE SOURDOUGH BREAD

2 cups dough starter
1 1/2 cup lukewarm water
4 1/2 cups flour
4 teaspoons sea salt
2 tablespoons oil

Combine dough starter, water, 4 cups of flour and salt in a large bowl and mix by hand until a sticky dough forms. Cover the bowl with a cloth and allow the dough to rest and rise until it is doubled in size. The time this takes will change according to the temperature of the kitchen. (Warmer areas, the dough will rise faster.) When the dough has risen, knead it by hand, adding in the last 1/2 cup of flour and sea salt. Knead for 10 minutes, then let it rest for 10 minutes. Shape into two loaves, let rise once more until doubled in size and bake at 400°F for 40 minutes.

* * * * *

HORSE BREAD

2 cups dough starter
1 1/2 cup lukewarm water
4 cups flour
1/2 cup cooked kidney beans
1/2 cup cooked green peas
4 teaspoons sea salt

Mix by hand the dough starter, water, salt and 3 1/2 cups of flour in a large bowl until a sticky dough forms. Cover the bowl with a cloth and allow the dough to rest and rise until it is doubled in size. The time this takes will change according to the temperature of the kitchen. (Warmer areas, the dough will rise faster.) When the dough has risen, knead it by hand, add in the peas and beans and last 1/2 cup of flour. Knead for 10 minutes, then let it rest for 10 minutes. Shape into two loaves, let rise once more until doubled in size and bake at 400°F for 50 minutes, test to see if it's done through by inserting a sharp knife into the dough; if it comes out clean, the bread is done.

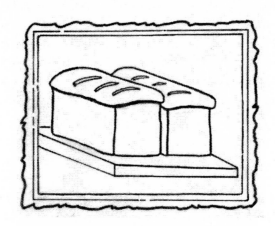

BREAD SOUP

4 tablespoons vegetable oil
8 large cloves garlic
4 diced turnips
6 diced parsnips
2 large onions
1 ham bone
Salt
Pepper
6 tablespoons molasses
10 cups water or vegetable broth
1 large loaf baked bread

Lightly sauté the garlic, turnips, parsnips and onions in the vegetable oil. Add the ham bone, water, salt and pepper and bring to a boil. Let boil for one minute, turn down the heat to low and simmer for 3 hours. Add the molasses and stir. Pour over slices of freshly baked bread to serve.

* * * * *

Mother thought of a special meal fitting to celebrate our first risen bread in the New World. She does love to bring people together over food. She says sharing brings good light to the heart.

Squanto offered a pheasant for the feast, informing Mother that pheasants are a most flavorful bird, but a little dry to the taste. It is best prepared with moisture added to the roasting.

We all set to work to help, knowing our reward was only hours away. As Mother prepared the pheasant stifle, Squanto and I made berry pye. Mary and Patience snapped the green beans. At length,

I asked permission to visit Father where he was building a new shelter. When I arrived, the men told me he had left an hour before. Baffled at his whereabouts, I headed for home, only to find him there. I did ask him where he had been. He smiled, a twinkle in his eye, and before we bowed our heads to give thanks for this special meal, he said that I needed to learn patience or my curiosity will be an affliction. I confess that my curiosity was an affliction. I so longed to know his secret, I scarce tasted the meal.

* * * * *

PHEASANT STIFLE

2 pheasants, cleaned, gutted and cut into pieces
3 tablespoons vegetable oil
2 medium onions, chopped
4 cups cabbage
2/3 cup apple vinegar
4 tablespoons sugar
1/2 cup chicken broth
12 juniper berries
Pepper
4 tablespoons oil or butter
Salt

Wash the pheasant and pat dry. Heat the oil in the skillet and brown the pheasant pieces. Remove from the skillet. Sauté the onion in the oil until nicely browned. In a separate bowl, mix the sugar, vinegar, stock, cabbage, berries and pepper. Lay the pheasant in a roasting pan, rub the pieces with oil or butter. Spread the cabbage mixture on top of the pheasant, cover the dish and bake in a 350°F oven for 1 1/2 hours. Test the meat and if the juices run clear, it is done.

*****

GREEN BEANS IN CIDER AND ROSEMARY

1 pound of green beans
3 tablespoons oil or butter
1 onion
1 tablespoon chopped rosemary
1 tablespoon cider vinegar
Salt
Pepper

Break off the stem ends of the beans and cook whole in rapidly boiling salted water until tender (about 7 minutes). Drain and cut into 1/4 inch slices. Heat the oil or butter in a saucepan, sauté the onions, then add rosemary and beans. Stir for one minute, add the vinegar and season with salt and pepper.

*****

BERRY PYE

CRUST:
3 cups flour
1 cup vegetable shortening or lard
1 egg
1 teaspoon white vinegar
1/4 teaspoon salt
3-4 tablespoons cold water
1 egg white for brushing crust

FILLING:
4 cups fresh berries
2 tablespoons flour
1/4 cup fruit juice
2/3 cup sugar
1/2 teaspoon cinnamon
2 tablespoons butter

TO MAKE THE CRUST: In a medium size bowl, sift the flour and salt together. Add the shortening and with your fingers, mix with the flour until the mixture feels grainy, like a coarse cornmeal. Mix the egg and vinegar together and blend into the flour mixture. Add just enough water so that the dough barely holds together, not sticky. Press the dough together into a ball and cover completely with a barely damp towel. Let it set in the refrigerator for an hour. After the dough has rested, roll it out with a rolling pin until it is about a quarter of an inch thick and line the bottom of a pie shell with half the crust.

TO MAKE THE FILLING: Clean and sort the berries. Toss with cinnamon. Mix the flour and fruit juice until smooth, add the sugar. Gently mix with the berries. Let the mixture stand for 15 minutes before it is put into the pie shell. Pour mixture into the pie shell, dot with the butter. Cover the pie with the top crust. Bake at 450°F for 10 minutes, reduce the heat to 350°F, bake for about 40 more minutes.

I was not the only one curious. Squanto, Mary, Patience and even Francis Billington, who had become a steady member of Mary's classroom and had joined us for supper, were much intrigued. After the last bite was consumed, but before we commenced the washing, Father asked Mother to close her eyes. He wanted to show her something. I thought this must be his secret!

Father led her, and indeed all of us, to an area in our back garden hidden by a stand of trees. Father told Mother to open her eyes. She knew what she saw, for she jumped with joy. "Tis a root cellar, I warrant!" she said.

Father raised the wooden door so that we could see the rough, wooden stairs that went into the ground. The earthy smell of the cave rose to meet us. The dirt walls were lined with shelves for storing our preserves for the winter. Soon the shelves would be full of dried, salted and pickled fruits, nuts, vegetables and herbs, stored in baskets, pots and burlap bags. I asked Father when he had made this, for he toiled with the other men house-building from sun up 'til sun down on all but the Sabbath day.

He said to me with a smile, "One hour a day, for many days, finishes a job."

July 1621...Summer Rain

Lightning continued to turn night to day for a flash, then all would be dark again. The thunder seemed to roll over us like a blanket and each clap brought rain so violent, the elders feared for our crops.

Squanto said t'was merely summer storms and we must take our share of rain, lest we anger God and he gives us less than our share. Squanto seemed to know our beliefs better than we! He had learned of our God from the Spanish priests who freed him and he seems to have forgotten nothing.

Mary, Patience and I huddled together inside the house and fair shook at every crack of thunder. We wondered would the skies ever end their outpouring. We sang nursery rhymes and songs we learned in Holland to soothe our nerves!

Finally we woke to quiet and realized the rain had ceased. We looked outside. Huge white clouds were moving across the sky and spots of blue could be seen. Rays of sunlight beamed upon the land! We ran outside without a thought to our boots which did get muddy, quite up to the ankle.

Melons ripen now as do strawberries, carrots and peas. Flowers bloom and give color to our lives such as we thought we would never see once we left Holland. The rains were a blessing and I shall not be afraid of them again.

Our stores of cheese from the ship's crossing were now gone and Mother set about to make cheese from the goat's milk and I was interested to be by her side.

* * * * *

CLABBER CHEESE

1 gallon fresh milk, room temperature
1/2 cup buttermilk
Water

Cover and let set 12 to 14 hours, until clabbered (when the curds and whey are separated and the curds are firm to the touch). Cut the curd into cubes. Let rest 10 minutes. Add 2 quarts very warm water. Heat but do not bring to a boil or the curd will toughen. Let it simmer at 100°F for about 30 minutes to an hour, stirring every 5 minutes. Do not break the curd. As the whey is forced out, the curds will settle.

Pour the curds and whey gently into scalded, porous cloth sack or triple layered cheesecloth. Rinse curds with COLD WATER to minimize acid flavor. Let drain in cool place until the whey ceases to drip. Keep the cheese cool till you are ready to serve.

August 1621...River Play

The weight of my skirt, apron and bonnet felt desperately uncomfortable and heavy this hot airless day. I walked slowly down the path to the stream as Mary and Patience trudged beside me. Mother had sent us to fill buckets with fresh water. We kept our mouths closed lest we expend our energy complaining about our discomfort for all of us had red, moist faces from the heat and humidity. But we did forget ourselves entirely when Blossom appeared as if by magic and fell into step beside me! Her long hair was straight and shiny, so different than ours, always stuffed under our bonnets. Her eyes were the shape of almonds and her skin toasted so that no sun could harm it. Mary and Patience could not stop staring with a bit of envy at her thin, sleeveless buckskin dress that hung freely on her. I attempted a conversation. It was halting but we did exchange words until I felt we understood a bit of each other's meaning. I vowed to learn the Indian tongue. It was indeed full of sounds that were of fascination. And as I stumbled on some pronunciations, Blossom and I laughed and

Mary and Patience joined in. We found young grapes on a vine and tossed them into one another's mouths and soon laughed, as if we were friends who spoke the same language.

At the water's edge, we each set down our buckets, our errand quickly forgotten by the lure of the water on this hot summer day. Undoing the buckles of our shoes and removing our stockings, we were all quickly standing to our knees in the swift, cold current, using our toes to grasp the stones beneath our feet. Blossom was more sure-footed and laughed as we slipped about.

'Twas a joy until that mischief Francis Billington shouted our names. Blossom, like a deer, bounded up the bank and into the woods. Francis came upon us and commenced to kick water in our direction. Mary and Patience ran for the opposite shore. I stood my ground and used my hands as great scoops to soak Francis Billington! With dismay, I realized that I did not soak him half as well as he soaked me. My clothes were soon heavy with water and Mary and Patience giggled at my state. Finally, to stop his splashing, I did retreat to the opposite shore where my sisters were and dared him to follow.

Patience called out loudly, "Do you dare soak your teacher, Francis Billington? She might be sure to fail you and turn you from her classroom!" At this, Francis blushed, muttered that he had work to do at the river and lifted heel and ran off. Mary chided Patience for calling attention to Francis' lack of schooling. Mary said she, in a way, admired Francis for his determination to learn all that he can. I, still smarting from the soak Francis gave me, retorted that Francis should learn how to be less of a nuisance.

From a short way up on the riverbank, from behind a tree, I heard laughter; a laughter too deep for Blossom. I was feeling wet, brave and sorely used and called, "Come out and show yourself instead of hiding like a sissy. It is rude to watch another without presenting thyself."

"Since I am no sissy, I will present myself with apologies," Samuel, a boy of my age, said as he stepped into sight. When I first met him on the Mayflower, I named him the "Scholar" for he always carried a book and when not working alongside his Father, spent his time reading. This time he clutched a fishing pole as well. The cowlick in his brown hair stood at its usual angle. I saw his blue eyes regard my wet demeanor with great amusement. He made a deep bow, "I do not mean to be rude, Constance Godwin, I meant only to say good day. I can see by your damp expression, it may not be a good time." Then he hoisted his line full of fish over his shoulder and retreated into the wood.

I was speechless. I did not know Samuel knew my name, at least he had never spoken it.

Patience warranted that I had made an impression on Samuel.

For my part, I wondered, with a sinking feeling in my chest, that it may not have been the best impression and would, hopefully, not be lasting.

Mary reminded us of our labors and we set about the picking of the blackberries. I tried to forget about the meeting with Samuel. But strange it was that his words played in my mind over and over. Finally I chided myself and determined to let visions of another of my mother's berry pyes tease my tongue. Of late, she has allowed me to prepare the crust, and taught me her secrets for pastry. Father says my meat pye shows I am truly my mother's daughter.

Later, as the pyes went in the oven, Francis arrived at our doorstep and presented a dozen catfish as apology. Am I imagining that Francis seems sweet on Mary? His eyes do stay on her and shyly asks for more of her help in his reading and writing as he has now for many weeks. Mary, for her part, did seem special concerned to be involved in the cooking of his gift of catfish.

I could not help but wonder if Samuel's catch of fish that day had been as bountiful.

* * * * *

CATFISH WITH CORNMEAL DUST

1 pound catfish fillets
One egg
1 tablespoon water
Salt
Pepper
1 cup of cornmeal
4 tablespoons oil or butter
2 large onions

Slice and sauté the onions in 2 tablespoons of oil or butter. Add salt and pepper and brown until flavorful. Take out of pan, set aside. Beat the egg with the tablespoon of water. Spread the cornmeal on a plate, season with salt and pepper. Dip the catfish fillets in the beaten egg, coat each fillet in the cornmeal, both sides. Melt the remaining oil or butter in a very hot skillet, sauté the catfish 3 to5 minutes on each side (depending on thickness) or until done. Put sautéed catfish on a platter, cover with onions.

CATFISH AND CORN

4 catfish, cleaned and cut into pieces
1 medium onion
1 cup stock
1/4 pound bacon
Salt
Pepper
2 cups corn kernels

Brown the bacon and remove from the pan. Brown the onions in a tablespoon of the remaining bacon fat. Add the catfish pieces and stock, cover and simmer for 10 minutes. Add the corn and simmer for 5 more minutes. Serve in bowls with bacon crumbled on top.

AUTUMN

September 1621...Acorns and Apples

Patience, Mary and I had settled under a tree in the hopes of improving our needlework. We sat on a hill and looked down on the men building a new shelter. I could see Samuel, already as tall as his Father, working alongside the men. Our only conversation was now embedded in my mind and I decided not to watch him. My eyes found my mother; she was approaching carrying a basket brimming with ripe crab apples. Happy to be so quickly lured from our sewing, we all rose to greet her. Eager hands reached for the bounty of the basket, but our mouths met with great disappointment.

The apples were small and sour but Mother, as usual, was determined to use this fruit to advantage. I was hard pressed to see how it could be made edible.

Mother decided to pickle the apples and she did assure us of her confidence that it would enhance our appreciation of the bountiful fruit. She bid us work in the cutting of the little wonders, unless we'd rather pursue the making of our quilts.

I did remember where I left my knife and quickly relieved Mother of the basket and headed for the house followed by Mary and Patience. Our needlework would remain idle for many days.

* * * * *

PICKLED CRAB APPLES

4 pounds crab apples
1 cup dried apricots
3 1/2 cups vinegar
4 cups sugar
1 teaspoon cloves
1 teaspoon cinnamon

Slowly heat the sugar and vinegar together over medium heat. Add the spices and diced dried fruit. Core, peel and dice the crab apples, add to the syrup. Bring the mixture to a slow boil, cook until the crab apples are tender. Store in jars or a heavy pot, serve with fowl, pork or as a side dish.

* * * * *

CRAB APPLE AND MAPLE SYRUP PUDDING

7-8 slices of bread, crusts removed
3 tablespoons lard or butter
1 pound crab apples
1/2 cup sugar plus one tablespoon
1 cup maple syrup
1 tablespoon cinnamon
1 teaspoon ground cloves

Line a deep baking dish with slices of bread that have been spread with lard or butter, spread side down, fitting the pieces snuggly together. Peel, core and slice apples and layer them into the bread-lined dish. Combine 1/2 cup sugar and spices, sprinkle mixture over the apples. Pour 3/4 cup maple syrup over the top. Cover the mixture with remaining slices of bread, spread with lard or buttered on both sides. Sprinkle the top with remaining sugar and rest of maple syrup. Bake in a 300°F oven for 2 hours. Serve warm with thick cream.

* * * * *

The end of September was so hot it scorched our pea crop, but now the days shorten and cool. There be no idle hands from sunrise to sunset as we pack salted fish and eel in barrels to ship back to England as part of repayment for our passage.

Squanto showed us how to gather acorns, brown shiny nuts with caps on them, which grow on oak trees. He says white acorns are sweeter and be less bitter tasting than red acorns. We collect them as soon as they fall, before animals eat them. He says they are best boiled so they lose some of their bitterness.

97

ACORN FLOUR

Fill a pot half full with acorns and fill the pot with water. Any acorns that float throw away (they are hosts to worms and are no good). The acorns that sink should be put in a big pot, cover with water, bring to a boil. Turn the heat down and simmer for 20 minutes to soften the shells. Pour off the water and let the acorns cool. With a hammer, crack the acorns side to side, not top to bottom. Hulls will break off. Return the husked acorns to the pot and cover with water once more. Boil for 20 minutes. Pour off dark tannin-covered water. Cover with fresh water and boil again. Repeat until no dark colored water results after boiling. Spread acorns on cookie sheet and bake for 2 to 3 hours. When kernels are dry and brittle, grind them into flour.

* * * * *

I must confess to the heavens I have developed a fondness for lobster. Try as I might, I cannot find a sin in liking this food, except the killing of the poor creature. My mother says the broth from the cooking of this animal is the secret to many of her dishes. I do believe her for this creature is the most tasty and succulent of all in the sea. The meat of the claws and legs certainly be delectable, but it is the meat of the tail that fills my dreams and can make me salivate when deep in sleep.

Today I watched Samuel fashion a lobster trap. He carried the trap to the shore and, after tethering it to a nearby tree, summarily sank it. He sat and quickly produced a book for the reading.

Patience found me observing him and did tease me that some girls may need more chores, for idle hands be playground for the work of the devil.

* * * * *

BOILED LOBSTER FOR ONE

1 and 1/2 pound live lobster
3 quarts salted water

Bring the water to a boil in a large pot. Drop the lobster into the pot, cover and boil for about 15 minutes. Retrieve the lobster, cut down the belly and remove the shell and eat.

* * * * *

LOBSTER AND CORN SOUP

1 pound cooked lobster meat
5 cups milk
2 cups corn tender
Salt
Pepper
4 tablespoons minced parsley

Bring the milk to a boil; add the corn, salt, pepper and parsley. Reduce heat and simmer for 10 minutes or until the corn is tender. Add the lobster meat and simmer for 2 more minutes. Serve warm.

October 1621...Pumpkin Harvest

The days grow so short. I wake in the dark and scarce get my chores done before I'm rolling out my bedding again!

November 5th will mark the 16th anniversary of Guy Fawkes Day. In England, much celebration undoubtedly will occur. Thinking of this reminded me of the yearly feast we had in Holland that was in celebration of the Dutch defeat of the Spanish in 1575. I made so bold as to ask Governor Bradford if we might want to celebrate our good fortune with a feast of our own. At this, Mother added that it could be a feast to bring people together in thanksgiving. He appeared thoughtful and solemn, as is his way, but then a small smile flickered across his face as he said to me, "Wise words from a young poppet."

Governor Bradford agreed with Mother that this celebration should include all our neighbors to let them know how much we thank them as well as the Lord. Thus, through Squanto, he sent word to Chief Massoit to ask if the Wampanoag people would join us.

With our day of rejoicing drawing near, all naturally turned to Mother for ideas and, finally, leadership. Preparing enough food for our entire community and the tribe of Wampanoag required much planning and the knowledge of cooking good enough for feeding the court of a king. Mother kept her pride in check, but did allow that she was fair excited for this honor. She had chores for us every day.

One clear morning, she had Mary, Patience and I follow Master Clarke to his bees to gather the honey to sweeten her baking. Francis Billington, blowhard that he be, walked along with us for a piece, bragging that anyone can train a bee, they be such small buzzing objects. When invited to show his prowess, he claimed, eyes downcast, that it was his day to watch the field. Was it my imagination or did he glance at Mary to see if she thought ill of him? If he hopes not, then henceforth, perhaps he will watch his boasts!

Master Clarke be a fearless bee charmer who can get the honey from the hive without garnering one sting! My adopted sisters and I were full of caution and hid behind a tree to watch him at his work. Patience giggled nervously, ready to submerge herself in the stream should the bees pursue her.

Happy we were to present Mother with that pail of liquid gold. "Aye, how sweet our pyes will be!" she exclaimed, hugging the three of us.

Mary did take me up short when she asked if she could speak freely with me, in private. I wondered what her topic might be and when we sat close together at the fire, I found out. She asked that I be not so harsh on Francis Billington. She said that Francis has a good heart, for when he is present during her schooling hours, he does encourage the younger students. She added that his own reading had progressed so much that his Bible was well-thumbed. Mary did accept that Francis could be a bit troublesome, but then she did blush and admit she suspected he was showing off for her benefit. That was a notion that she found heart-warming! I laughed, hugged her, and told her that I would endeavor to remember Francis's good qualities and hold my tongue when he did provoke me. I admitted that Francis did have a way for the growing of the pumpkins. Only the day before, he ceremoniously presented his largest to Mother who was quite delighted. It was large enough for young Oceaneus to bathe in, I warrant! Mary, Patience and I laughed at the thought of seeing the baby who was born on the Mayflower taking a bath in a pumpkin shell. We came up with this poem:

"For pottage and puddings and custards and pyes
Our pumpkins is the favorite supply
We have pumpkins at morning and pumpkins at noon
If it were not for pumpkins, we should be undoon."

*****

PUMPKIN AND HAM STEW

3 cups diced pumpkin
6 cups stock
2 tablespoons vegetable oil
2 medium onions, chopped
1/2 pound diced ham
1 cup corn kernels
1 teaspoon salt
1/2 teaspoon pepper
Toasted pumpkin seeds

Put the stock, pumpkin, onions and oil in heavy soup pot. Cover and simmer for about 15 minutes. Add the ham and corn and cook until corn is tender. Season to taste. Pour into bowls. Top with toasted pumpkin seeds.

* * * * *

SWEET ROASTED PUMPKIN SEEDS

Pumpkin Seeds
Maple Syrup
Maple Sugar
Vegetable oil

Wash the seeds and dry them. Place them on a large heated frying pan with oil, toast until they show a few tiny brown spots on the husk. Let them cool for 5 minutes, then toss in a small amount of maple syrup, just enough to lightly coat them. Sprinkle maple sugar over the seeds and toss. The sugar will keep them from sticking together. Cool.

Eat as snack or put into soups.

PUMPKIN SOUP

2 two pound pumpkins
2 large onions, chopped fine
2 tablespoons vegetable oil
8 cups stock
Salt
Pepper

Peel the pumpkin and remove seeds. Dice the peeled pumpkin and set aside. In a large pot, brown the onions in the oil. Add the pumpkin, stock, salt and pepper. Cover and cook until thick and smooth, about 2 hours.

* * * * *

ROASTED ONION AND PUMPKIN

10 pumpkin slices
1 onion
2 teaspoons rosemary
1 teaspoon salt
1/2 teaspoon pepper
2-3 tablespoons vegetable oil

Slice the pumpkin and onion, put in bowl. Cover with herb, salt and pepper and oil. Toss so vegetables are well-covered. Place on baking sheet and bake at 350°F for 30 minutes or until well-browned.

* * * * *

FILLED SUGAR PUMPKIN

Cut the top off the pumpkin and clean the cavity of its meat and seeds. Keep the pumpkin meat and seeds separate.

3 cups cubed sugar pumpkin meat
3 eggs
1 teaspoon ground cinnamon
1/2 teaspoon ground ginger
1/2 teaspoon nutmeg
1 tablespoon molasses
1/2 cup maple syrup
Apple juice

Mix all the ingredients and fill the pumpkin shell. Cover with the pumpkin lid and place in a baking pan. Bake at 350°F for 1 to 1 1/2 hours or until the mixture has set like a custard.

November 1621...Friends and Thanksgiving

As the plans for the Harvest Celebration continue, Mother keeps a long list to remind herself of all the details. How does she keep from being frantic with it all?

No one is spared Mother's attention with the assignment of chores. The youngest child capable of helping was put to work, plucking berries and bringing them to her in baskets. Boys and girls shuck and shell the corn, pick mussels from the shallows and dig clams. Every woman in the village seems to know her duty and helps in the effort, from cooking to finding herbs. Still others make clam shell spoons for the eating of the soups Mother loves to conjure.

God be praised, the men provide enough game and fish to suit Mother's fancy. Samuel, book in the pocket of his pants, approached Mother to ask how many lobsters she desired for the feast. She was most pleased with his politeness. For my part, I was surprised when he offered to share his latest book of the plays of Shakespeare with me. My face felt hot as I admitted I do like reading and find it even more enjoyable to read a book chosen for my delight by another. I accepted his kindness, but allowed how Mother keeps us too busy to spend long hours reading. He enjoined that the moments I could steal would be well worth it. Samuel left to his lobster gathering and I placed the book among my most treasured things.

The ovens are readied and kept hot with fires going for days as we prepare. The fragrance of fish soups, meat stews, succotash, and roasting venison and pork fill the air.

* * * * *

PORK AND CABBAGE

Preheat 375°F

1 1/2 pound pork tenderloin
Salt
Pepper
2 tablespoons fresh thyme
2 onions, sliced
4 turnips, cut into inch pieces
Vegetable oil
3/4 cup maple syrup
1/4 cup fruit juice (apple or cranberry)
1/2 cup diced uncooked bacon
4 cups chopped cabbage
3 tablespoons brandy
4 tablespoons vinegar
1 cup water

Grease a baking dish with oil, add the cut turnips, drizzle maple syrup atop. Cover the baking dish, bake at 375°F for 20 minutes. Take the cover off and cook for another 10 minutes or until turnips are tender. Set aside.

Sauté the bacon in a large sauté pan. Add the cabbage, cook for 3 minutes. Add the brandy and vinegar and cook until the liquid is nearly gone. Add water and cook until the cabbage is tender. Remove the cabbage and reserve the cooking liquid.

Season pork with salt and pepper and thyme. Place the onions in a roasting pan, lay pork on top. Roast at 450°F for ten minutes, lower temperature to 350°F. Cook for 30 minutes or until pork reaches 150°F internal temperature. Let it rest for 10 minutes.

Put the cabbage and turnips back into the oven to warm while you add the remaining liquids from the vegetables together and heat. Place cabbage and turnips on a platter, place pork atop. Spoon sauce over.

* * * * *

Today is one day before the thanksgiving celebration and all are filled with excitement. Mary and I were collecting water and saw two of our men catch ducks at the riverbank's edge. As we had seen Squanto show them, they quickly split each duck's neck for the bleeding while it was warm from life. Squanto says the blood and bad humor leaves the ducks' bodies quickly this way and improves the cooking. We let our presence be known and hastened to take the fowl to Mother, who bid us pluck them as she was ready to roast them on the minute.

Squanto silently stepped in next to Mother, as was his way, and lent assistance. He rinsed the birds with two palm-fulls of whiskey. He nodded at Mother as she chose three birds to roast on a spit. She placed an onion in their cavities to draw off any ill flavors. She gave the task of turning the spit to one young lad and told him to keep the ducks moving over the fire. The lad felt important for his assignment. I wonder if he still felt quite so satisfied after hours of turning the birds over a hot fire.

As Mother readied a marinade, Squanto broke the breast bone of the other ducks, explaining that this made the ducks easier to cook and eat. The breast of wild fowl was usually its best part, the legs being tougher and full of tendons. I must confess I had only had duck once before in my life and remembered it as being greasy and good for the making of soap.

Squanto gave me his quietest smile and warranted I wouldn't feel that way about these quackers after he helped Mother prepared them.

* * * * *

MARINADED DUCK

1 duck, cut into pieces
1 medium onion
2 bay leaf
3 cups whiskey or brandy
1 teaspoon pepper

Combine onion, bay leaves, whiskey, pepper and pour over the duck pieces. Be sure the liquid covers the meat. Let stand in refrigerator for 48 hours. Remove bird and dry. Save the marinade.

Put 4 tablespoons of salt pork or vegetable oil in casserole dish, brown and then roast the duck pieces for about 1 hour at 375°F, turning several times. Strain the marinade and pour it over the pieces. Return to the oven for 30 more minutes or until tender. Salt to taste.

* * * * *

ROASTED WILD DUCK

2 wild ducks, cleaned and plucked
Salt pork
1 medium onion

Cover the ducks with salt pork for the meat is very lean and needs this extra fat. Place ducks on a rack in a roasting pan. Roast at 500°F for 20 minutes, reduce heat to 350°F. Remove the salt pork and roast 20 minutes

* * * * *

BRAISED WILD DUCK

1 wild duck, cut into parts
4 tablespoons salt pork or vegetable oil
1 large onion
4 turnips
1 teaspoon oregano
1 teaspoon tarragon
1 teaspoon chili powder
Salt
Pepper
1/4 cup brandy
Water to cover

Heat the oil or salt pork in a cast iron skillet. Salt and pepper the duck parts, place in the skillet and brown on both sides. Add onion, turnips and herbs, brandy and water. Simmer, covered, 25 to 35 minutes or until duck is tender.

* * * * *

GINGER DUCK BREAST

4 duck breasts
1 tablespoon ground ginger
Vegetable oil
Salt
Pepper

Add salt, pepper and ginger together and rub over duck breasts. Brown breasts in oil in a heavy oven-proof skillet. Place skillet in oven at 400°F for 20 minutes.

Thanksgiving Day

The day of the feast has arrived!

I think all pots in the entire community are filled with food. Men have cut planks to use as serving boards. Barrels are full of fresh beer and declared ready.

Mary, Patience and I woke early and peeped out the window to see Mother and others in our village already outside, seeing that the fires were laid and that all would be ready when needed. So, we were not the only ones who had risen early, excited for this day.

All wondered when the Indians would arrive.

We dressed and ran out to help Mother but she was discussing a pottage with the women, so we turned our attention to a morning meal.

What to eat the morning of a great feast? Mary teased me, saying I was one who was never too excited to eat!

It was then that Samuel appeared at our house, delivering dozens of lobsters. He mentioned that he was fancying popcorn for breakfast, which sounded appetizing to me as well. As he did look at me expectantly, I suggested we prepare the popcorn over the fire that had recently been lit in the garden. Mary and Patience kept me company, sending me looks that were filled with meaning, which I did not appreciate. I did tell them I could manage with Samuel on my own well enough, thank you. But they stuck to me like tar as I watched Samuel put a layer of sand in a clay vessel and hold it over the fire. When the sand became hot, he removed the vessel from the heat and poured the kernels of corn into the hot sand. He stirred the sand as if conjuring a potion. As the popped kernels rose to the top, he easily removed them and put them in a bowl for me. I bid him take some for himself and he said he would, if we could then eat in companionship.

Mary and Patience giggled and hurried off. Feeling my cheeks flush with embarrassment, I hurried inside to bring out maple syrup and a bit of cream to pour over our popcorn. We found a patch of sunlight where we could eat. The taste of the breakfast I do not remember, only the worry of thinking of things to say and the concern of being spied with maple syrup on my chin. Mary and Patience remained close by, glancing at us much more often than was necessary. Sisters! God bless them for, at the moment, I surely could not.

I had little time for feeling contrary. Mother asked me to see to some of the preparations for she could not be in more than one place at a time.

Samuel took his leave, saying we were sure to cross paths at the celebration. I nodded, at a loss for words. Mother called again and I ran to her. It felt good to have a purpose so as to move my thoughts away from Samuel's companionable breakfast. Mother said she needed to trust me to be her eyes and ears today to make sure all was cooked and ready. I did say that I hoped to be her nose as well, for the smells were most inspiring!

Off I went to see the seating area. The tables and benches for the men folk were in alignment. Trenchers were stacked. Napkins folded. All looked to be ready.

Now, I wondered, would our guests arrive?

* * * * *

SLOW ROASTED SALMON
AND TURNIPS

2 pounds salmon, cut into filets
1 large turnip, peeled and cut into round
   slices
1 large onion, sliced
2 cups stock
Vegetable oil
Salt
Pepper

*Season salmon with salt and pepper and rub
with oil. Place the cut turnips and sliced onions
in a greased baking pan. Roast at 250°F for 20
minutes.*

* * * * *

The sun rose high in the sky and still no sign of
our Indian guests. Men and boys played games,
women talked and stirred their pots, girls made
dolls from vines and hay and we waited.

Presently, Governor Bradford enjoined every
man, woman and child to come together. Though
there was no sign of the Wampanoag people, he
thought it time we joined hands and raise our voices
in the singing of a psalm. That is when we heard
the sound of others approaching!

Ninety feathered men came into our midst
followed by women and children!

They had arrived!

Many among us took deep breaths. Never before
had we seen so many Indians together and so many
more than were expected.

Although they brought deerskin bags filled with
kernels of corn, I heard Mother confess to Father

her worry that we would not have enough food. Chief Massasoit was quick to see our deficiencies and within the hour of his arrival, dispatched his people to get more food. They returned with five deer, many wild turkeys, fish, beans, squash and berries.

Now we had more than enough. How could we cook it all? How could it all be eaten?

How fascinated I was to see the Indian women sit at table with their men! Their eating customs be much different from ours. Squanto and Samoset said that although it was usual for Indians to eat upon furs or mats upon the ground, the tables were acceptable. He did misunderstand me, for I did not think it unusual for the women to sit at table, but for women to sit in the presence of their men-folk, which a woman of our community would never think to do.

This made me realize that customs are not the same in all places, or with all people.

I have looked for Blossom, but there be many people and I still have much work. So, alas, I haven't seen her.

By nightfall we realized our guests were prepared to stay as long as the merriment continued, for they did roll out their beds. I saw Mother and the other women notice as well and realize that the celebration was to continue into the morrow. I must confess I wanted the excitement to continue as well!

Day Two of the Feast

At dawn I ran out to ensure the fires were still hot and saw Samuel and the men return to camp with fresh felled deer. God forgive me, I suffered jealous feelings that I will never know what it is to go on the hunt because of the petticoats I wear. Squanto has described the hunt for food to me as a grand adventure. He tells me that a deer that is killed quickly with no chase, as is the Indian way, will be tender and easy to cut as bear grease. How I would love to creep stealthily through the brush, not snapping a twig, to see my prey and know I will feed my family. Enough of this dream spinning; I must to the river for water!

As I set out with my buckets, I heard the music playing and saw some folk set to dancing. I kicked up my own heels knowing I could jig a bit upon my return.

* * * * *

ROASTED VENISON

6-8 pounds venison roast
Salt
Pepper
2 teaspoons dried oregano
2 teaspoons dried sage
2 tablespoons minced garlic
8 tablespoons oil or butter
2 medium onions, chopped
1 cup brandy
1 1/2 cups dry red wine

Brown the garlic and onions in 2 tablespoons of oil or butter in a roasting pan. Add the sage, oregano, salt and pepper. Rub the remaining tablespoons of oil or butter evenly over the venison roast and salt and pepper the meat then add it to the roasting pan. Roast at 450°F for 20 minutes, reduce the heat to 325°F and add the brandy and wine and roast for about 12 minutes a pound. Remove the roast to a platter and cover to keep it warm.

* * * * *

VENISON STEW

Venison meat
2 medium chopped onions
1/4 vegetable oil
8 cups vinegar
4 cups water
3 bay leaves
1 tablespoon thyme
1 tablespoon basil
1 tablespoon ground cloves
1 tablespoon ground allspice
1 tablespoon crushed peppercorns
1/4 cup flour
1 turnip, diced

Sauté one of the onions in the oil. Add the rest of the ingredients. Simmer for 1 hour. Strain and cool. Marinate the venison for 12 to 48 hours in the refrigerator. Turn it every once in a while. Dry the meat and dredge in flour. Brown the venison in salt pork or vegetable oil. Add marinade to cover meat by an inch, turnips, remaining onion. Cover and bake at 375°F for 2 to 3 hours or until the meat is tender, turning meat a few times as it bakes. Add additional hot marinade or boiling water if the liquid level gets too low. When the meat is tender, pour off excess fat and serve.

* * * * *

The men killed three more turkeys, which we quickly readied for the hot water dip to ease the plucking. The joyous sound of the fiddle does ease our labors! How I wish Blossom were here that I might get to know her better and share this time with her.

* * * * *

ROASTED TURKEY AND DRESSING

12 pound turkey
2 cups cubed and dried-out bread
2 cups cubed and dried out cornbread
1 tablespoon oil or butter
1 cup diced onion
1/2 cup diced carrots
1/2 cup diced pumpkin
1 teaspoon dried tarragon
3/4 teaspoon salt
1/2 teaspoon pepper
1/4 cup melted butter
1/4 cup finely chopped walnuts
2 beaten eggs
1/2 cup dry sherry

Wash and clean out the cavity of the turkey. Make the dressing: sauté the onion, carrots, pumpkin in the tablespoon of oil or butter. Add the salt, pepper, nuts and tarragon and set aside. Put the breads in a large separate bowl, add the beaten eggs and sherry, then the vegetable mixture. Finally add the oil or melted butter and mix thoroughly. Stuff the turkey cavity with the dressing, tie the turkey legs together. Rub the turkey with a mixture of vegetable oil, salt and pepper it generously.

Place in a 450°F oven for 20 minutes, reduce heat to 350°F and roast for approximately 4 hours or 16 minutes a pound.

* * * * *

TURKEY HASH

2 cups shredded roasted turkey
1/3 cup diced parsnips
1/3 cup diced carrots
1/3 cup chopped onion
3 tablespoons oil or butter
1 teaspoon thyme
1 tablespoon maple syrup
1 cup turkey gravy
1/2 teaspoon salt
1/4 teaspoon pepper

Sauté the onion in oil or butter till brown, add the parsnips and carrots, salt and pepper and sauté till tender. Add the thyme, maple syrup, gravy. Add the turkey meat, season to taste. Warm the meat with the rest of the ingredients and serve.

* * * * *

TURKEY STIFLE

2 cups cooked turkey
6 tablespoons oil or butter
1/2 cup sliced squash
1/2 cup sliced carrots
1/2 cup sliced onions
1/2 cup corn
1/2 cup cubed pumpkin
Salt
Pepper
1/4 cup maple syrup
2 cups vegetable broth
1 cup cubed cornbread

Lightly sauté the onions, carrots, squash, pumpkin, corn in 3 tablespoons of oil or butter. Season with salt and pepper. Put half of the mixture into a greased baking dish. Layer the turkey on top of that mixture. Put the remaining half of the vegetables atop the turkey. Drizzle maple syrup and pour broth over this, then arrange the cubed cornbread on top of the entire dish. Melt the remaining 3 tablespoons of butter and drizzle over the top of the cornbread. Bake at 350°F for 25 minutes. Serve warm.

* * * * *

Day Three of the Feast

This feast continues to put joy into the cool days as winter comes upon us. Even though we women folk cook and clean from sunrise to moon rise, we feel happiness in our hearts. The men and boys have been playing with the Indian men at shooting the bow and arrow. They do hand wrestling and have other contests of skill as well. Our poor lads cannot beat them in running or climbing, however hard they try.

Even with our toil, we have had much pleasure. Mary, Patience and I each thrust a stick into an ear of corn and propped it over the fire. Some morsels fell to the fire, as some will, but what fun we had catching those white puffed kernels as they popped from the cob! I even caught one right in my mouth!

Francis Billington witnessed our revels and came to join us. I warrant he was desirous of being near Mary. I thought a bit of teasing might be in order, when Samuel appeared at my side! Mary did look deep in mine eyes and silently we agreed to a truce, for Patience was there as chaperone. There would be no sisterly teasing this day!

How we all did laugh when Miles Standish organized a parade. He had a drummer and a trumpeter who played with great enthusiasm, but little skill. Men mocked at being soldiers and carried their rifles, which they shot freely. Children banged whatever pan they could find that we weren't using for the cooking.

Just as the parade was ending, I did catch sight of Blossom and she of me. We did quickly move toward one another and started talking at the same time. This made us both laugh. Surprised I was that she had learned more English. She said she had asked Squanto for his help and he did oblige.

She did happily join me in the cooking, which continued with good cheer. I did my best to express my gratitude and thanks to Blossom and her people for their help and friendship. I lifted my eyes to God in thanks as well.

*****

CRANBERRY SAUCE

1 pound fresh cranberries
1/4 teaspoon cinnamon
1/4 teaspoon allspice
1/4 teaspoon cloves
1 cup maple syrup
1/4 cup brandy

Spread the cranberries in an iron skillet with a cover. Drizzle maple syrup, brandy and spices over them, cover and cook over low heat for an hour. Serve over cornbread or turkey.

* * * * *

MAPLE CARROTS

4 pounds of carrots
1 tablespoon vegetable oil
1/2 cup maple syrup
1 teaspoon salt
1 cup apple juice

Cut the carrots into two inch pieces and place in boiling water for 10 minutes. Put into a baking dish that has been greased with the vegetable oil. Bring the remaining ingredients to a boil and pour over carrots. Bake at 300°F for one hour, basting 4 or 5 times during the process.

* * * * *

CRANBERRY MAPLE PYE

CRUST:
3 cups flour
1 cup vegetable shortening or lard
1 egg
1 teaspoon white vinegar
1/4 teaspoon salt
3-4 tablespoons cold water
1 egg white for brushing crust

FILLING:
2 cups cranberries
1/2 cup maple syrup
2/3 cup apple juice
2 tablespoons melted butter
2 tablespoons cornstarch

TO MAKE THE CRUST: In a medium size bowl, sift the flour and salt together. Add the shortening and with your fingers, mix with the flour until the mixture feels grainy, like a coarse cornmeal. Mix the egg and vinegar together and blend into the flour mixture. Add just enough water so that the dough barely holds together, not sticky. Press the dough together into a ball and cover completely with a barely damp towel. Let it set in the refrigerator for an hour. After the dough has rested, roll it out with a rolling pin until it is about a quarter of an inch thick and line the bottom of a pie shell with half the crust.

Combine all ingredients and fill the bottom crust of prepared pie shell. Cover with top crust. Bake at 450°F for 10 minutes, reduce heat to 350°F and bake another 30 minutes.

MOCK MINCE PYE

CRUST:
3 cups flour
1 cup vegetable shortening or lard
1 egg
1 teaspoon white vinegar
1/4 teaspoon salt
3-4 tablespoons cold water
1 egg white for brushing crust

FILLING:
1 1/2 cups raisins
4 tart apples
1/2 cup apple cider
3/4 cup sugar
1/2 teaspoon cinnamon
1/2 teaspoon cloves
3 tablespoons cubed white bread, crusts removed
1 tablespoon brandy

TO MAKE THE CRUST: In a medium size bowl, sift the flour and salt together. Add the shortening and with your fingers, mix with the flour until the mixture feels grainy, like a coarse cornmeal. Mix the egg and vinegar together and blend into the flour mixture. Add just enough water so that the dough barely holds together, not sticky. Press the dough together into a ball and cover completely with a barely damp towel. Let it set in the refrigerator for an hour. After the dough has rested, roll it out with a rolling pin until it is about a quarter of an inch thick and line the bottom of a pie shell with half the crust.

TO MAKE THE FILLING: Pare, core and slice the apples. Combine in a saucepan with the raisins. Add the cider. Cover and simmer until the apples are very soft. Add the sugar, spices and bread. Add the brandy. Fill the bottom crust with the filling, cover with a top crust. Bake at 450°F for 10 minutes, reduce heat to 350°F and bake another 20 minutes.

December 1621...A Year Completed

December 25, 1621

Today I do reflect on my first year in the New World. I remember the meager dinner of last Christmas aboard the Mayflower, and happily eat my dinner of venison, pickled vegetables and fresh pudding. When my body does remember the rocking and cold of that boat, I hold my hands near the flame of our very own hearth, here on solid land. Though we lost many friends who traveled here with us, we have made many new friends.

I have overheard the Elders say that, even with all our efforts, we have not put by enough food to last the winter. But I know, by the grace of God, we will survive and even thrive in this new land.

* * * * *

MAPLE CANDY IN THE SNOW

Maple sap is cooked down to a very thick syrup stage. Pour the syrup on the snow in thick stripes or in fun patterns. It hardens immediately and you have a great chewy natural maple candy. Today you can reduce real maple syrup by boiling it to 270°F (do with a candy thermometer). Drizzle the syrup on snow or crushed ice cubes or on a cold cookie sheet that you put back in the freezer. You can even write your name!

LANGUAGE NOTES

Some of the words used in the Colonial Period are not words we use in everyday conversation today. Remember when Governor Bradford called Constance a "wise poppet" for thinking of organizing a celebration with their new Indian friends? **Poppet** is an old English word. It was used to refer to a doll or to one who was dear to your heart. Remember when Constance called Francis Billington a "younker"? That's another word that is not used much today. **Younker** means "young man."

Another word you might not be familiar with is "shallop." Remember that the Pilgrims used a shallop to get from the Mayflower to the shores of the New World? **Shallop** is a small open boat that can be used in shallow waters. You can use oars in a shallop or you can use a sail. When your shallop is on shore, it would be wise to "tether" it to a tree. Remember when Samuel was careful to tether his lobster trap to a tree so it wouldn't float away? **Tether** is a rope or a chain or something that you can use to secure a boat or an animal or a trap to a certain spot.

One of the dangers of traveling to the New World was becoming unhealthy on the ship during the long voyage. "Scurvy" is a disease that some Pilgrims suffered, and mostly because of their diet; a lack of fresh vegetables and fruit. **Scurvy** can cause your teeth to come loose and your gums to become spongy. If you add Vitamin C back into your diet, scurvy can be cured. The Pilgrims had to be careful that the food they stored would not get "contaminated." **Contaminated** means that food has become spoiled or poisoned by contact with insects or germs or anything that could make food no longer safe to eat.

There are lots of words for food used in the Colonial Period. Food was also called **edibles** or **victuals. Harvest** is a word used to describe the gathering of crops. When a harvest is large, it is called **bountiful. Ingredients** are the varied food items that are used in a recipe. **Forage** is a word used to describe the search for edibles that might grow wild. Many of the Pilgrims' meals, especially on the ship, were cooked on a **brazier.** This is a pan that holds burning coals or wood and has a wire grill on top. The food is exposed to the heat when it is put on the grill.

Constance's clothes were made of cotton and wool. Blossom's clothes were made of **buckskin,** which is the skin of a male deer. The skin would be washed in the river and then hung to dry in the sun. The skins would be cut into sections of a dress or a shirt or pants and then sewn with a needle made of sharpened bone.

The way Constance and her friends spoke during the Colonial Period is very distinct and true to its time. Many of the words Constance used we still use today. Many have gone out of fashion.

Author Biographies

JULE SELBO

Jule Selbo has written numerous screenplays including *Hunchback of Notre Dame Part Deux,* "Jacques' Story" in *Cinderella Two* and *Hard Promises.* Her television credits include: *Young Indiana Jones Chronicles, Life Goes On, Melrose Place and PBS' Misadventures of Maya and Miguel.* Her plays have been produced in New York, Los Angeles and regional theatres. Her short stories have appeared in *Alfred Hitchcock Magazine.* She received her Pro Chef certificates from Epicurean Cooking School in Los Angeles. She teaches writing at California State University at Fullerton, AMDA and UCLA Extension. She lives in Pasadena, California with her husband and daughter.

LAURA PETERS

Laura Peters worked for the Renaissance Pleasure Faire for several years before moving to Francis Coppola's Zoetrope Studios where she worked on such films as *Apocalypse Now, The Black Stallion* and *One From the Heart.* She has raised three daughters and her short stories and poetry have been published in the 2003 and 2004 editions of *Direction,* a literary magazine. She currently lives in Southern California on a boutique vineyard with her husband, is active in education and environmental issues and is pursuing a degree in organizational psychology.